CW00866217

THE DEVIL CALLS

Casey Denby

Chapter 1

"The only way I can describe Cass is..." I shuffled my scribbled notes, haphazardly lining them up. I tried to come to terms with the fact that I was stupid enough to think that describing my dead best friend as 'weird' at her funeral was appropriate. I glanced up, my face flushing as the words dried up. I saw Cass's mum, Leanne, trying in vain to stem the flow of uncontrollable tears that were streaming down her face like rain on a car windshield. I can't describe her as weird, I thought, Leanne doesn't want to hear that.

"Unusual," I finished lamely. As if that was any better. I saw Dad shake his head in disbelief and mum hid her face behind her hands. That wasn't off-putting at all. Neither was the fact that Cowan had also just face-palmed. I ploughed on, ignoring them, ignoring the sudden tightening in my stomach. "I know that's probably not what you would expect to hear her friend say, but I promised her that I would be honest if she ever-" Stop. That moment two weeks ago, when the two of us were sat on her bed watching Cowan throw a fit at another lost video game battle. Her face suddenly filled my vision, announcing, "If I ever die, can you guys be honest at my funeral?" She was curling a ginger hair around her finger, "Like, can you not pretend that I was perfect? Because I'm not. No one is and I don't get why people pretend so hard to be,"

What did I say back? I can't even remember. I'm pretty sure Cowan only grunted. Did he remember her saying that? Or was I the only one who felt obliged to do it?

I looked out at the crowd, a sudden stage fright enveloping me. Mum, Dad and Cowan shared a mixture of disbelief, support, and sadness. Cass's dad wasn't doing

3

much to comfort his wife since he too had dissolved into tears. There were a great number of prominent people attending the funeral too, such as Huang, a renowned doctor from the hospital and the Chief of Police along with a multitude of councillors. That was weird. Although Cass was known, she wasn't particularly liked. She was known as 'that odd girl from Church Croft'. Even Cameron Berkeley, the mayor's wife who shared the skin of a tangerine, had made an effort to show her face. Blake, her son, stood moodily at the back, tapping his fingers agitatedly on the wall whilst his sister, Courtney, was dabbing her heavily made up eyes with a handkerchief.

It all seemed a bit surreal. There I was, speaking at my best friend's funeral, to a bunch of people who never truly cared for her.

"Anyway," I coughed, regaining my composure, "what I'm trying to say is that Cass wasn't perfect, although she was perfect to me," I added quickly at the sight of Leanne's face crumpling, "And she was perfect to her family and-" I crushed my little cards that contained a perfectly normal speech into the palm of my hand, embracing fully the art of improvisation.

"And, even though she, er, didn't um-" Embracing the art of improvisation was possibly the worst decision I could have made at this point, "See herself as perfect, she was-er…" What's another word for perfect? Faultless? Unflawed? The opposite to not perfect? "Perfect. Thank you."

I leapt down the two steps, wanting to get back to my seat as quickly as possible. In my rush, I managed to trip and smack my knuckles with a resounding crack on the edge of a pew. It seemed to echo around the church as the Vicar resumed his preaching of a 'better place' before introducing our headteacher.

I sank low in my seat between Dad and Cowan, hiding my crimson face in my hands. "I s'pose it wasn't that bad of a speech," Cowan whispered, "I mean she was going to call you a clumsy oaf, wasn't she?" Cass's matter-of-fact voice repeated the words in my head: "If you die, I'm gonna be honest. You're a clumsy oaf. You're seventeen and your Dad still makes you use plastic beakers instead of glasses," she turns to Cowan, "And you, don't get me started. You can never keep still! You're hyperactive!"

"Weren't you hyperactive?" I asked nonchalantly, rubbing my reddening knuckle.

He chuckled softly. Dad elbowed me in the ribs, the universal sign for 'Shut up, he's staring at you,' Looking up, I saw Mr O'Donnell was glaring at me. Whether this was due to the fact that I had just given the worst funeral speech of all time or because I'd caused Cowan to start shaking with laughter would remain a mystery.

Mr O'Donnell's words started worming their way into my receptive senses, "I am deeply honoured that I have been asked to speak today. My heart goes out to Mrs Hawthorne and her husband as I can't imagine what they're going through,"

I could see Cass as she was in many assemblies, head lolling back, eyes closed and fake snores emanating from her throat. Cowan quietly faked a snore in my ear which caused me to snort. Even though it was funny thinking about her, it was still difficult. My eyes were starting to burn.

"She was a hardworking pupil who was always conscientious and worked to a high standard,"

"What is this?" Cowan muttered, "A frickin' monitoring report?" I squeezed my eyes shut to stop them watering and smiled. Cass was anything but hardworking. She never handed homework in or did her work in class. She deemed it a waste of time.

"She was an important part in our school community, a beating heart of communal spirit who motivated other students and was a friendly face amongst the crowds,"

"That's complete and utter rubbish," I whispered, trying to keep my voice from shaking too obviously, "She hated everyone. She rarely spoke to anyone else unless they spoke to her," As horrible as that made Cass sound, it was true. She couldn't be described as a social butterfly because she found everyone else totally shallow. They weren't able to understand the world like she did. Neither did we but apparently we didn't make it as "flipping obvious".

"Despite being a quiet student, she took an active part in assemblies and her classes,"

"She'd hate this," Cowan murmured, "He's not being honest in the slightest," he paused, "Do you want to go outside?" he asked when he realised I was crying. All I managed was a nod before he led me out the double doors into the cool October air.

"Green car!"

"That doesn't count, that's your car and it's been parked there the entire time," my voice was slowly returning to its normal pitch again after my crying fit, "You're still at one,"

Cowan's eyes were still red and a bit puffy too, but he was trying his very best to appear masculine by tactically facing away so I couldn't see, "I don't think it's fair that you chose silver cars. You should have chosen an obscure colour too, like pink,"

"Don't blame me for your bad colour-choosing skills please. Thirteen," I counted another silver that was blatantly speeding. We were sitting on the crumbling wall that represented the perimeter of the graveyard. It was the only part of the wall that was clear enough to sit on. The rest was either covered in ivy and brambles or was completely overrun by the forest behind the church like the entire west side of the graveyard.

I kicked my heels at the wooden sign beneath us, causing blue paint to rain on the ground. You could only just make out the words: St. Mary's Church and Raven's Wood. People draped in black started emerging from the church. Another condition Cass had set us was that we had to wear colourful clothes to her funeral if she died. "I don't want you all to be in black," she had said, "I want you guys to be bright. Black does nothing for me," Cass rarely wore anything but black. We had tried our best on this, both of us sporting colourful socks (mine were blue with pink spots whilst Cowan's were orange, an ode to Halloween pumpkins). We both knew it wasn't to the standard Cass would have wanted.

Dad wandered over morosely, his hands buried in his pockets. Mum stood a little way behind, smiling comfortingly. She seemed out of place in her black dress, I was so used to seeing her in paler colours. "It was very nice, the end, y'know," Dad said, "It's sad that you missed it,"

"Really?"

He shrugged, "Well, no," he conceded, "I didn't know who did the song and that headmaster of yours wouldn't shut up,"

"I thought you liked him,"

Dad shrugged again, opened his mouth to say something, but then scratched his nose instead.

"Are you coming for lunch?" I asked.

He shook his head, "No, I can't after all," He wasn't looking at me, instead watching the Chief of Police chatting to one of the councillors, "I have to go to a meeting," He didn't look particularly thrilled. If anything, the prospect of this meeting seemed to worry him.

The four of us had planned to go out for lunch. Dad had said he probably wouldn't be able to make it, but I was still disappointed that he wouldn't be there. As well as being Cass's funeral, it also happened to be my birthday. I was eighteen today. It also meant that I would have to pay for my own birthday lunch. Great.

"Drive carefully Cowan. Keep my girl safe,"

"Sure will,"

Dad ambled over to the chatting men, his hands still having not ventured out of his pockets. Mum waved and followed him, standing close as Dad began to chat away wearily to the Chief of Police, Mr O'Donnell and Huang. She had obviously chosen against lunch too, but I couldn't blame her. Busy, crowded places made her nervous.

Cowan and I watched silently as the graveyard and carpark began to empty. Leanne was still crying, great sobs wracking her whole body. Mr O'Donnell folded himself up in order to fit into his electric car and drove away as if the devil himself was after him. Eventually, the only car left was Cowan's lime green one.

"Well, this is the suckiest birthday ever,"

"We were planning something you know," Cowan said after a moment of silence, "It was gonna be awesome. In that old barn that nobody goes near so that we could actually drink a lot and nobody would care. I have two Piña colada mixes, a rum, and three vodkas hidden in my room. Mum's gonna think I'm an alcoholic," my heart contracted in my chest as he trailed off and mumbled, "She was so excited for it,"

We waited longer still, talking about Cass as if she had only just gone on holiday or something. It was weird to think of it like that, to think that we were never going to see her again. What had happened will possibly remain the most traumatising event of my life. No one should go through what she suffered. But, I thought as I counted the fourteenth silver car to speed by, I hardly thought about that. My mind was filled with memories of her and acted as if she was still around. That morning I had found an old photo album of when we were small, (Cass was rocking a great ball of wiry ginger fuzz, Cowan still had his baby fat and I looked like a boy) and my first thought was: 'Oh, I'll have to show Cass that'.

They had found her body over a week ago, why was she still hanging around?

"Do you think," Cowan interrupted my reverie, "That she knew?"

"Knew what?"

"What was gonna happen?"

"How'd you mean?" I asked, faking confusion but knowing exactly what he was getting at.

"Don't you think it's odd that she would suddenly start talking about her funeral three days before she went missing?"

"Coincidence," I said stoutly, "There's nothing else to it,"

"But Mel-"

"No."

He carried on anyway, stubbornly ignoring my protests, "That's her all over though," he said, "It's exactly like her to know something like that,"

"You know I never believed any of that," I responded, rubbing my eyes. They were starting to burn again, a sure sign that tears were coming, "She knew I never believed it,"

"Just because you didn't believe it, doesn't mean that it wasn't true," he pushed.

I gulped, "Forget lunch, I wasn't hungry anyway," I jumped down from the wall and stormed away, heading towards home. Before I knew it, I head his engine kick into gear and gravel flying as he hurtled out of the carpark. He pulled up beside me, winding the window down manically.

"Go away Cowan!"

"Melanie, don't you walk away from me,"

"Watch me," I muttered.

"Mel, I didn't mean to upset you," he called, narrowly avoiding mounting the curb, "I just need you to listen. Something's happening and I don't understand it. I should have explained it to you before,"

My turning was coming up, an alley cut through. It would take me longer to get home, but at least I wouldn't have Cowan following me the whole way.

"Or, at least, I should have started by explaining it better,"

I just shook my head, quickened my pace.

"Mel please, I really need you right now,"

I turned into the alley, throwing him the middle finger in response.

Chapter 2

"In retrospect, you reacted terribly to that situation," Mum said as she fiddled with a loose thread on my duvet. We were reflecting two hours later on what Cowan had said. I mumbled an incoherent response. I had to agree, I had been unreasonable. My rage had lasted one hour and a half in which time I had walked for forty nine minutes, managed to get changed, made a mess of the kitchen and my bedroom and angrily eaten a banana (which did not have the desired effect of demonstrating my anger as an apple possibly could have). It wasn't Cowan's fault. Whenever I thought of Cass in that way, it made my insides wring themselves into a tight knot.

When Cass said that she wasn't normal, she wasn't joking. Ever since she had moved next door ten years ago, she had insisted that she could see ghosts. At first, I thought she was joking, then I thought it was an attention-seeking thing because she was all a bit out there anyway with her bangles and her frizzy ginger hair, and then I just accepted that it was part of who she was. I never really believed that she could. Although in the end I conceded that perhaps there was something to it because she just knew things. Things that she shouldn't, things that I didn't like to think about. She always said that's what she liked about me so much.

"We were destined to be friends you know," she'd announce, "But you know what makes it a hell of a lot easier? That fact that I like you Melanie. I like how you're honest, because you don't pretend that you believe me, you outright tell me that you don't,"

"That's because I don't," I'd respond every time.

I sighed and sat up, "I don't want to talk about that sort of thing though," I said, an unmistakable whine in my voice.

"You can't hide from these things Mel," Mum looked at me and she seemed weak and faded in the late afternoon sunlight, "Sometimes, you have to talk about them with people. You have to talk about the difficult things,"

"But why?"

She sat in silence for a minute of two, winding the thread around a skinny finger, "Because you owe it to her. You have to accept her, and I know-" she held up a hand as I opened my mouth to argue, "you think you have or had. But you have to open yourself up to this now and let it in like Cowan seems to have done. You can't get left behind,"

I buried my head in my knees and refused to look her in the face, "Getting left behind is so much easier,"

To my surprise, Mum laughed. She rested a hand on the back of my head and stroked my hair, so lightly that I could barely feel it, "Don't worry sweetheart, you're already half way there,"

"Thanks Mum,"

"It's okay sweetie," she got to her feet and moved towards the door, "Now get some ice on that knuckle, it'll take the bruising down,"

I nodded, staring at my knuckle that was undergoing its transformation from red to blue. Cowan was right, it was too much of a coincidence that Cass spoke about her funeral three days before she went missing. Considering how much she talked about dead people, Cass never really liked to talk about death itself, especially her own. I thought about Cowan's last words to me: 'something's happening and I don't understand it'. As Mum disappeared down the landing, I jumped off my bed and, gracefully tripping on the discarded black dress I'd worn to the funeral, and bounded down the stairs to the phone.

Just as I reached it, it trilled and I picked it up hurriedly, fumbling with it in my fingers, "Cowan?"

"No, this is Dad,"

I rested my forehead against the wall, burning with embarrassment, "Dad,"

"I was calling because you didn't answer your mobile so I guessed you'd be home. Looks like I was right, yeah?" he said loudly. He always shouted into the phone, never quite grasping the concept that the greater distance didn't mean he had to shout louder.

"Uh yeah,"

I could still hear the laughter in his voice as he said, "Did you go for lunch then?"

"Um no, we're going to-" I dragged the word out as I tried to think up a convincing lie, "go later, or more precisely now because we thought that it would be a good idea to uh," I stumbled over my words, speaking slowly to give the rarely used deceptive part of my brain more time to think, "Get changed!" I almost shouted as inspiration hit, "We thought it would be a good idea to get changed and then go so that we could freshen up and sort ourselves out. That's why I thought you were Cowan," I finished, thinking I was tying the lie up quite nicely, "Because he said he would call,"

"You didn't have an argument or anything?"

"What?" I sounded incredulous, "No! What made you think that?"

"You're terrible liar Mel, I'll catch you later,"

"Yep, seeya Dad," I sighed with relief as he hung up and then nearly wet myself as the phone rang again, "Dad?" I guessed.

"No, this is-"

"Cowan,"
"I really need to talk to you,"
"Okay, I'll come over,"
"Oh, you don't need to," he said cheerfully, "I'm already in your driveway,"

Chapter 3

Twenty minutes later, I sat at Cowan's kitchen table. I absent-mindedly tapped my fingernails against the table top, tracing the grains and knots whilst an icepack balanced precariously on my other hand. Cowan was making two cups of tea and was rattling around in the cutlery drawer, searching for a spoon. The chaotic clatter barely drowned out the white noise in my head as I tried to make sense of was he had told me.

"You still don't believe me do you?" he sighed, placing the tea in front of me.

"Nope,"

"Right..."

"It just doesn't make any sense! How is it even possible?"

He shrugged.

"It's not, that's why. It's, it's," I grasped for some sort of explanation and managed to come up with: "Hallucinations! That's it! You're just seeing things,"

"Then why are you still here?"

It turned out Cowan knew me better than I wanted to admit. He had been steadfastly silent on the way to his house because he said that what he wanted to tell me would most likely cause me to freak out and he didn't particularly fancy crashing his car. When we got to his house (literally, about three minutes later) he told me, as calm as you please, that he was seeing Cass.

I know right? Classic Cass. She dies but sticks around like an overzealous baby sitter.

If I were to be honest, I would have immediately responded with "I totally believe you," because I did. The thing was, although Cowan and I had been friends since I could remember, Cass and Cowan didn't always get on. Cowan's relaxed, somewhat cautious, and low-key nature didn't always match Cass's ultimate, life-threatening plans. I didn't want to admit the resentful thought that was smoking at the base of my skull: how come Cass had shown herself to Cowan and not me?

I was still there because I wanted to see Cass again.

"I'm still here… because…" I tried to think up a convincing lie. The only lie that came to mind was 'for the tea' but that was pretty shameful, even for my standards. I stopped trying. My inexplicable aversion to telling Cowan the truth became outweighed by a need to understand. I opened my mouth to admit my thoughts when Cowan's face suddenly changed, drooping limply in horror. His knuckles turned white as he gripped his mug and stared.

"What?" I demanded harshly.

He held out a finger that trembled slightly, pointing at the fridge. I looked from him to the fridge and back again, "Cowan, there's nothing there!" I snapped. Talk about melodramatic. Yet, that fear at the base of my skull suddenly bloomed into thousands of doubts, the largest pulsing like a sunbeam: Why couldn't I see her? What was wrong with me?

The sudden scrape of his chair made me jump as he leapt to his feet, throwing himself at the back door, "She's gone outside. She's heading across the garden, to the tree," At the far end of Cowan's garden was an old, gnarled oak. Apparently it had been there since the 'good ol' Witch Hunting Days', but none of us believed those tales anymore, even when Cass insisted that they had used the tree for hangings. Its branches were as thick as

Roman Columns, stretching powerfully towards Raven's Wood and the church in the distance.

Cowan skidded to a stop and I copied a short distance behind him. I'd seen the look on his face. He was staring at that empty space with such longing it made my heart crack. It made me realise something that I had been ignoring for the past few months.

'Me and Cowan will catch up with you in minute, awright Mel?'

Sure.

'I just really need to talk to Cowan, Mel, you know? Alone?'

It was suddenly blatantly obvious. I felt like I didn't belong, as if I was third-wheeling. I took a few more steps back, letting him have his privacy with my dead best friend that only he could see.

Gee, life could be unfair.

I watched silently as he muttered, "C'mon, what are you trying to show us?" He ran a hand through his hair and turned to me and waved me over, he seemed to have got a grip on his raging hormones, "She's right next to the tree, staring at it,"

"Just staring at the tree?"

"Yes,"

"Just... staring?"

He looked at me, annoyance beginning to creep across his features, "Yes, for the last time, she's staring at the tree,"

I started moving towards the tree, still holding his gaze, "So, let's go have a gander at where she's looking at,"

He nodded assertively, "Good idea," It wasn't until I reached the tree that I realised he had only taken a few steps before stopping.

I didn't bother to say anything, simply rolling my eyes to emphasise my disapproval at him wimping out. I investigated the tree trunk. There wasn't anything out of the ordinary, just the usual deep-set wrinkles and crevices that was a home to the fungi and moss. This had been the place to go when we used to concoct our Witch's potions. There was nothing scratched into the bark, or tied to it, or anything that could attract Cass's attention.

I shrugged at Cowan, "There's nothing here,"

As I said it, my throat constricted and I started to cough. A sudden cold breeze caressed my arms with icy fingers. I couldn't seem to get a breath and my head started to loll on my neck, losing its usual, familiar weight. My body rolled, twisting and my feet were being gently lifted away from the ground. My vision was pulsating almost, my blood hammering against my forehead. It was so slow, then-

"Mel!"

I was hanging by my neck from the oak tree. I tried to scream, clutching and scratching at my neck, my entire body spasming in violent cravings for the air. My blood hammered harder, my vision blacking in and out. The last thing I saw through the fuzziness sneaking in at the corners of my vision was Raven's Wood and Cass, beckoning.

The first sound I woke to was the crashing of glass and Cowan swearing. I rubbed my forehead first before opening my eyes, trying to soften the throbbing in my head. When I eventually did, I found myself on Cowan's sofa in the den, watching Cowan as he tried hopelessly to sweep up a smashed glass with a dustpan and brush. Hot steam from a of mug of tea floated in tendrils across my face. I sat up, swaying slightly and watched him a bit longer.

When he saw me sitting up, he jumped and smacked his head on the heavy, wooden cabinet, causing him to swear again, "You scared me," he said reproachfully, "Quit laughing,"

I hadn't even realised I was smiling, "What are you doing?"

He smiled sheepishly, "Raiding the liquor cabinet,"

"Why?"

"Isn't whisky good for fainting?"

"I thought that was brandy,"

He shook his head, "Sorry, all we have is whisky," at which he pulled a bottle out the cabinet, un-stoppered it and poured a glug into my mug, "Don't tell your Dad," he whispered conspiratorially. I picked up the mug and took a sip. Despite the high tea to whisky ratio, it still burned on the way down and not because it was hot.

"What about the rum upstairs?"

"Don't be dumb, rum's not good for fainting. Jeez, pick up a book," Cowan was staring at me as he sat down at the other end of the sofa. Like, uncomfortably hard staring.

"What are you looking at?" I asked, self-consciously.

How beautiful you are.

"You look terrible," was all he said.

"Wow Cowan, you really know how to compliment a girl,"

"No seriously, what the hell happened? Look at yourself," He held a mirror up and I nearly choked on the tea. Cowan was right, I did look awful. There was an angry blue and purple bruise forming like a choker (adequately) around my throat. There were nasty red blood marks as well where the skin had broken. I was pale. Translucent. Practically ghost-like.

Oh and emotionally traumatised.

"Mel, what happened?" he asked softly.

Could I tell him? How in hell could I explain to him that I had just relived the last few moments of an innocent woman hung from a tree for witch crimes that she hadn't committed? I felt like I had just died. My stomach flipped over as I thought about Cass. Is this what she went through? Cass's reason for death hadn't yet been confirmed, basically because no one knew how. Her body had been a mess when it was discovered. Blunt head traumas, stab wounds, evidence of strangling. It was impossible to tell what had killed her. And of course, no one knew who it was. It made me sick and I had to take deep breaths before I could say anything.

"I saw Cass," I said softly, deciding on probably the least upsetting part of my experience, "She was beckoning me over to Raven's Wood," I didn't elaborate on how I could see Raven's Wood from his garden. Standing at the base of the Oak, you couldn't see beyond the hedge of the adjacent field.

"I suppose that's where we'll head then," Cowan decided. He stood up, heading towards to the hall.

"Wait, now?" I scanned the outside street through the window anxiously. Dusk was beginning to fill the street. It was the sort of darkness where you saw everything through a blue filter and only the things in your peripheral vision were in shadow. How long had I been out?

"You want to wait?" he asked disbelieving, raising an eyebrow.

"I want to go when it's light,"

"I'll get you a scarf,"

What?! "Cowan, Cowan no!" But he'd already gone.

Chapter 4

"Oh, this is a brilliant idea!" I said, with as much sarcastic cheerfulness as I could muster, "Let's go to the graveyard in the woods in the middle of the night!"

Cowan rolled his eyes, "Just shut up and peddle,"

Cowan was standing on his bike, pedalling just a little in front and to the right. His legs were slowly rotating to a deliberate, regular rhythm whilst mine were careening around like suicidal windmills. I was struggling to keep up. I had originally agreed with the idea of going on bikes, but we only got half a mile before the half packet of biscuits I'd devoured in a nervous fit of hunger before we left caught up on me.

Cowan cycled back for the car, grumpily demanding why I hadn't gone and eaten the entire packet, and we'd parked it half a mile away and cycled the rest at Cowan's insistence due to the original reasons: it was much less obvious than showing up in a car, we could still out cycle any running human (in case someone did try to chase us) they wouldn't be able catch us, etc. It was as if he was expecting us to run into someone.

Whilst gasping for breath and with burning legs, I decided that even if there were people there who's attention we didn't want to attract, I would have preferred the car and to hell with being subtle.

We cruised down the final stretch and wheeled into the carpark, wincing as my brakes squealed.

"You want to make any more noise?" Cowan hissed. Then he rolled onto the gravel, the stones scraping and grinding against one another which broke the silence with a greater strength than I did.

"You want to make any more noise?" I responded, sarcastically. I was exhausted already and my neck felt like it was on fire.

We hid the bikes between the wall and the hedge, pushing them, rather short-sightedly, as far as we could into the thicket. We followed the grass verge that snaked next to the wall, heading towards the wood that looked suitably creepy. We crept together, supporting one another because every now and then one of us would slip on the damp ground.

We eventually reached the edge of the wood after sneaking past a sea of slowly decaying gravestones. "Let's do this then," Cowan said, flicking on the torch on his phone and aiming it at the ground.

It wasn't so bad at the beginning. The trees were spaced quite far apart to make room for the graveyard that over spilled its original boundaries. Graves leaned at odd angles, only held up by the ivy that had embraced it in a suffocating hug. It was deathly silent. Any of the birds that usually hung around here had roosted; there was no breeze so the trees weren't moving. It was eerily still, everything frozen, waiting in an inexplicable anticipation that I didn't understand. Particles hung in the air, unmoving, and I felt as if we had stumbled into some sort of netherworld.

"Where exactly are we heading for?" I asked in a whisper. I felt guilty for disturbing the peace, as disconcerting as that peace was, "I mean, Raven's Wood is pretty big,"

Cowan shrugged, pointing vaguely "Over there somewhere?" The vague direction he was waving at was the deepest part of the woods, beyond the graveyard where the unconsecrated ground was. Where there were hundreds of bodies buried, unmarked except for a few abandoned stone graves. It was as good a place to start looking as any.

Without us realising, the trees closed in. They leaned over us, creating a canopy, and the darkness didn't fall gradually. It was sudden and the only light was the circle created by Cowan's flashlight. I was quickly tiring and my heart kept fluttering in fear at Cowan slipping or sniffing. "Where are we even going?" I complained, whining, and I resorted to the classic: "Are we nearly there yet?"

"Will you shut up for just a… a minute!" Cowan hissed, his shoe losing its grip on the muddy ground for the thousandth time.

"Why?" I demanded, somewhat hysterically, "I'm sick of getting bitch slapped by trees!"

Cowan suddenly switched the light off just as I lost my footing. I scrabbled wildly, arms wind milling, and caught his elbow and he helped me regain my balance. I prepared to shout at him when he pointed through the trees. There was small golden glow that flickered distortedly through the needles of the pine trees. Cowan and I moved forward slowly, gripping one another, "What exactly are we s'posed to do?" I asked, my heartbeat beginning to speed up.

"I don't actually know,"

"What?!"

"We'll just watch what's happening for a bit and then we'll go," he said it as if it was easy and, most of all, safe.

"No, no, absolutely not!" I hissed, clutching his arm.

He moved ahead of me, pulling away, "C'mon, it'll be fine,"

I remained stubbornly where I was, arms crossed. I stared hard at the flickering glow. Every two or three seconds something crossed in front of it, plunging it into darkness for a second before it reappeared. It wasn't hard to guess that it was people crossing in front of it that was causing the rhythmic light, dark, light, dark.

"Cass would want you to do it,"

Now that was low. "Cass isn't here though!" my voice was wobbling again and, for that moment, I hated Cowan for putting me in this position and I hated myself for being so useless, for being so scared and cowardly.

"Please Cowan, let's just go. This isn't right," I started backing away. I could barely see his face in the darkness and it took me a second to realise that he had turned his back on me and had continued forward anyway. Asshole.

It was hard waiting. I was trapped in the pitch black, pine trees caressing my back and arms as I jiggled up and down to keep warm. It hadn't been this cold when we came. I could just see my breath, blooming like smoke directly in front of my face. I focused on the glow and the systematic dark, light, dark, light. My breathing began to match it, regularly in, out, in, out. I gradually calmed, my tense shoulders relaxing and my weakened knees strengthened.

It was some time later, when my fingers were blue and my nose was burning from the cold, that I figured something was wrong. That regular switch between the dark and light of the glow had stopped. The people, or whatever they were had stopped moving.

It'll be fine, I told myself, Cowan would be back any second, any second now...

There was a snap to my right, like fingers clicking. I jumped out of my skin, whirling around to face the direction of the noise. My brain couldn't keep up with what was happening, it had only just concluded that it was someone treading on a twig after I saw the shadow standing five feet away. They were half hidden behind a tree and my body worked faster than my brain, slowly backing away whilst whispering, "Cowan?"

Then something else came crashing through the undergrowth like a furious wild pig. I stumbled backwards, moving faster away from the shadow and away from, what I suspected was, the wild pig. Naturally, I tripped over my own feet and landed with a thump on my back, smacking my head on a rock. I swore, scrambling to my knees as the shadow lunged forward and manifested into a figure in a black cloak. Clearly not Cowan. Their hand stretched out and grasped the scarf. It happened in slow motion, and I saw his hand in clear detail: tendons creating ridges on the back, dry and chipped nails with individual particles of dirt trapped under each one… And then the scarf pulled taut and the world came rushing back at full speed.

I was being strangled. Again.

The next few seconds blurred into one another. My heart pounded as, in a panic, I scrabbled at the scarf. Then the furious pig came closer and was revealed to be Cowan. One second I was rolling in the mud struggling to breathe, the next Cowan was on the floor next to me, on top of the cloaked figure who was now clutching the scarf in a veiny hand and then Cowan was pulling me roughly to my feet and was throwing me forward. It took me a few steps to get a grip of my balance, but when I did, I took off running.

Cowan's breathing was ragged behind me, and it sounded weird, as if he was some distance away like on the other side of a glass pane. I didn't dare look round though, for fear that my feet would suddenly do their own thing and I would face plant.

After a traumatising amount of time getting whipped in the face by branches and scratched by thorns, we burst out onto the main path. The gravel sprayed from beneath our shoes as we pounded towards the forest edge. I could just see it, through the thinning trees.

I heard Cowan whimper and then he called to me, sounding as if he was still behind a wall of glass. In fact, everything seemed to be subdued, "Whatever you do, don't turn round,"

Of course, I glanced over my shoulder and squealed, "What the hell did you do?" Following us were three figures in large black cloaks that billowed out behind them, one covered in mud and now wielding an... an axe? Are you actually kidding me? They didn't even seem to be running, but gliding and they were gaining. I had flashbacks of how terrified I used to be by the appearance of Voldemort in the first Harry Potter film. They had an uncanny resemblance.

"I may have... interrupted a ritual... or something," Cowan gasped. I could tell from the look on his face that he was just as scared as I was, "They were dancing... around the fire... chanting,"

"Are they frickin' devil worshippers?" I cried.

"I think so," was his only response before he gave an extra burst of speed and dove into the bush containing our bikes. When I had caught up, he was already crawling out screaming at me to run, "I can't get 'em out, just run. We'll run to the car,"

I barely missed a step. As we clattered onto the road, the cloaked figures pounded through the gate. They were running in time to one another and they didn't seem to be out of breath or anything. Oh crap, I thought, What the hell have we got ourselves into? Cass, what happened to you?

We sprinted down the centre of the road. I didn't think I would be able to make it. I'll be the first to admit that I'm unbelievably unfit. But glancing back gave me all the motivation I needed. My adrenaline would spike and I'd fly.

Cowan reached the car before I did, fumbling with his keys to unlock it. He still hadn't managed to unlock the doors when I reached the passenger side, and I did a nervous jig whilst screaming at him, "C'mon, c'mon, c'mon Cowan!"

"I'm trying, I'm trying," I couldn't believe it, but Cowan had tears streaming down his cheeks.

The three figures had slowed to a walk, threateningly. As Cowan still hadn't managed to unlock the doors, I decided to change tact.

"You're doing great Cowan, you've got ages. Just take your time, it's fine," This calmed him and he finally managed to get the key in the lock and twist. We leapt in, slamming the doors and hitting the locks. He turned the key, and hit the accelerator. And stalled.

He froze, "I've forgotten how to drive," he gasped, the tears still streaming.

"No, you haven't idiot!" I shouted, "Put it into fricking gear!"

"Clutch down gas off," he mumbled under his breath, "Clutch down gas off,"

The cloaked figures had caught up and were trying to open the doors. I didn't dare look at them, my bladder was hurting too much and I didn't trust it. Cowan gently pressed on the accelerator, but the engine was groaning nastily and we still weren't going anywhere. Or we were, just really slowly.

"What am I doing wrong?" he screamed, "I don't know what I'm doing! I'm in gear, I don't understand!"

"Handbrake!" I yelled, thrusting it down. Just as we lurched forward and stalled again. The third figure brought the axe down, smashing the rear windscreen. I don't think I've screamed as loud since. Cowan bellowed, "That's my car!" and restarted the engine, his gift of driving suddenly returned to him. We lurched forward again, but thankfully didn't stall. I promptly put my seatbelt on as we hurtled around the corner, leaving the axe-wielding maniacs in our dust.

We sat in silence for a few minutes, catching our breath, just staring at the road as it rushed through the headlights and underneath and past us. Then suddenly Cowan started chuckling, which caused me to start giggling and, with the wind blowing around the inside of the car, we laughed hysterically.

"I forgot to drive," Cowan gasped, "What is wrong with me?"

An unbidden memory emerged in my mind from a few months ago. Cowan was driving and I was riding shotgun, both of us oblivious to the fact that Cass was hiding in the backseat. We had been chatting about him just having passed his test when he suddenly started shouting, "Oh my God, I've forgotten how to drive! I've lost control, we're gonna crash!" whilst flailing his hands about.

It only lasted a few seconds and he was being funny, but it just caused me to scream manically at him, "Drive you idiot! Stop mucking around!" He laughed at my reaction, far too heartily for my liking, "You'd know I'd never crash with you in the car," he said softly.

Which was the exact moment that Cass decided to pop up like a dodgy horror movie, demanding, "What about me?" She caused us both to jump violently, Cowan jerking the steering wheel which made me shriek again. He managed to not land us in a ditch as we both recovered our breath.

The memory made me smile, thinking of the three of us as just care-free teenagers where the worst things in our lives was the amount of schoolwork we were drowning under or the fact that our favourite TV character had supposedly died but we wouldn't find out for sure until March.

"You know there are Satanists in Raven's Wood, Mel,"

"Sure thing Cass, absolutely,"

"No, seriously, I've seen them. Performing rituals and shizz,"

"I bet,"

Cass's words hit me like a steam train, "She knew!"

Cowan flinched, "Pardon?"

"Cass knew that there were people, devil worshippers or whatever, in those woods,"

A moment of silence as Cowan comprehended what I said… "What?"

I quickly explained, asking if he remembered the conversation (which he didn't) and whether or not he agreed with me, to which I only got a mumbled "I've already said that," of which I ignored.

"Ugh, I need time to think about this," I said. I was finding Cowan's grumbled responses unhelpful and I could tell he wasn't really paying attention, he was continually glancing in the rear mirror at his windscreen. Cass's words were running round and round my head, "I've seen them," What did it mean? Did they have something to do with her death? Accidentally joining a devil cult sounded uncomfortably like Cass, what with all her charms and belief in magic. I thought of the condition her body was found in, and the axe that the stranger had been wielding jumped unbidden into my mind. I suddenly felt sick.

When we pulled into the drive, somewhat windswept, the clock on the dashboard slowly turned over to 1:17.

We sat for a while, just staring at the garage door, comprehending how our evening had unfolded.

Then Cowan began talking to himself, "Oh crap," he muttered, "Oh crap, oh crap, oh crap,"

He tumbled out of the driver's seat, tangled in his seatbelt and he flailed helplessly for a moment before I clicked the belt and released him. He half crawled, half ran around the back of the car and ran his fingers through his hair in despair.

"What am I s'posed to say?" he moaned, staring hopelessly at the destroyed windshield, "Oh sorry Mum, some Satanists tried to kill us and it was them who put an axe in the back window,"

"I feel like we have more pressing matters," I said as I clambered out from the passenger's side, lacking the vital sympathy that Cowan was craving, "Like, the fact that they know exactly who the car belongs to because it's so bloody vibrant!"

"Please do not take your stress out on my car. It's not his fault,"

"Oh for God's sake," I ignored his frantic mutterings about replacements and headed straight for the kitchen, making sure the back door was locked as I put the kettle on. I sat at the table, watching it boil, and sitting on my hands to stop them from shaking. It hurt my bruised knuckles but that seemed the least of my problems.

Cowan wandered in, engrossed in his phone and absentmindedly getting the hot chocolate from the cupboards.

"Did you lock the front door?" I asked.

"Mm,"

"I locked the back,"

"Oh, good,"

"I think I'm going to have a heart attack, Cowan, and die because I'm so scared right now. Aren't you scared too? I mean, what did you see? You saw something that was so much worse than what I experienced. How are you okay right now? Cowan? Cowan!" I groaned, "Cowan, are you even listening? I'm going to have a heart attack!"

Cowan was on his phone, ignoring my tirade, "Oh, that's great," he said cheerfully.

"What? What can possibly be so great about this?" I demanded.

"The car repair place's phone line is open 24hours,"

That shut me up, "This is so surreal,"

"Why?"

"Half an hour ago we were being chased by Satan-worshipping murderers and now you're on the phone to car repair people. What the actual hell?" Hysterical laughter bubbled up inside me again and I buried my head in my hands, "What is happening? What has my life become?"

Cowan was steadfastly ignoring me, his grin bordering on the insane as his phone rang. I got up and left the kitchen, unable to stand his optimism and his ability to take his mind off disturbing events. I found myself in the hall and decided to call Dad. As I bought up his number, I got distracted and stared at my reflection in the mirror. The red rawness of my throat was lessening but, if anything, the bruising was getting worse. As well as that, I had lost Cowan's scarf.

It was just as I was leaning in close, inspecting a particularly gruesomely green area of my bruising when I saw Cass. I froze. She was standing, staring at me, without expression. This couldn't be Cass, could it? Cass's face always had some sort of feeling to it, there was always a light behind her eyes. But now, nothing. I half expected an

Insidious moment, where I would turn around and she wouldn't be there and when I turned back to the mirror... well, you know the rest. I didn't dare take my eyes off her.

She was dressed like she was the last time I saw her. Stripy leggings, mini-skirt, a floaty top and her favourite denim jacket covered in a chaotic range of buttons and patches. There was no evidence of her death. My chest constricted. I missed her so much.

I watched as she slowly pointed at my phone that was lying on the side-table where I had left it, and slowly shook her head.

Chapter 5

I sat at the breakfast table the following morning, following my regular Saturday morning routine of sharing a coffee with Mum but I was in zombie mode. I acted as if nothing was wrong, as if I hadn't stumbled through the door at 6:36am, after a patchy clean-up of the cut on the back of my head and roughly a four hour sleep on Cowan's couch. I left early, annoyed when he didn't tell me what he had seen. Mum was flicking through the newspaper dreamily. She used the tips of her fingers to turn the pages over slowly, as if she didn't really want to touch the paper.

"They've found two old bikes squished into a hedge up by the church," she said, "Looks like the belonged to a couple of teens,"

It was hard to cover the fact that my heart had just dropped to the bottom of my slippers, "That's in the newspaper already?" I asked, trying to match her casualness whilst my knuckles turned white around my coffee mug.

"Already? You mean you knew about it?"

Crap.

I shook my head quickly, thought for a moment, and corrected myself by nodding and giving a weird, lop-sided shrug, "I heard some guys were going up with video cameras, trying to get some spooks on record," I wriggled my fingers at spooks, making light of a situation that I was finding to be very, very heavy, "Must have got scared and scarpered,"

"Melanie, I'm your mother, you think I don't know what you get up to in the evenings?"

I'm pretty sure you don't.

I relented, admitting that Cowan and I had cycled up to the church. I hated lying to Mum, especially since she was so fragile, so I decided I would simply fail to mention certain aspects of the evening. Such as nearly getting killed.

"Rather short-sighted, wasn't it?" she concluded.

"Yes, especially since the bikes got left," I shrugged and busied myself making another coffee to avoid any other questions. That was the wonderful thing about Mum though, she never pushed a subject I didn't want to talk about. She just offered small pieces of advice.

That was around the time Dad came in. He slumped into a chair at the head of the table, heavy bags under his eyes. Mum said "Good morning dear," and he simply twisted the newspaper around to face him. I frowned and he looked at me bemused, "What are you scowling at?"

"Nothing," Mum sighed and drifted out and a few minutes later the pipes started to creak, indicating that she was running a bath.

Dad began reading the same article that Mum had, and asked the same sorts of the questions. I managed to fend off most of them with the original lie, that it was some kids from school trying to catch ghosts. It seemed to rattle him, but he eventually accepted it, unlike Mum. They rarely spoke to one another anymore, so it was unlikely that the inconsistencies between my stories would be noticed. I wasn't sure if that was a good thing or not.

The cooker clock now glowed 8:56, my head felt like someone had squeezed too much cotton wool in so it was now pushing against the front of my head.

"Are there any 'spooks' down by the church?" Dad asked a few minutes later.

I shrugged and gave a non-committal grunt, gulping down a swig of coffee. I decided I wouldn't say anything, , but that was after my mouth had started talking, "There's so many rumours about round there though, you know? Like, Satanists and devil worshippers and stuff,"

Oh my God, what are you doing, stop talking.

"People just scare one another with stories like that, the history club use them as initiation or something," I sighed with relief as the rush of speech diarrhoea eased.

From the tone of his voice, Dad didn't seem bothered; he'd already changed the subject which easily confused me in this state.

"You stayed at Cowan's last night right? Not Courtney's?"

"Why would I stay at Courtney's?" it came out a bit more indignant than I meant it to.

"I thought you were friends?"

"Nope, not really. Barely talk to her actually,"

"You should," he turned a page slowly and deliberately, "Nice girl. Howard is always saying how you and Courtney would get along swell,"

I rolled my eyes, he'd been talking to Howard. Howard Berkeley was Courtney's father and he also happened to be the mayor. Big man, lots of power. Dad and him were "best mates". Apparently. I couldn't shift the feeling that Dad didn't like very much either.

"Since when did you start listening to Howard?"

"Since-" he was cut off by the shrill ringing of the phone.

We sat there for a moment, listening to the phone screaming at us to answer it and put it out of its misery. Then I heard Mum call from upstairs, "Mel, can you get that?" I stood up, and Dad almost leapt out of his seat and we both hurtled down the hallway. I still reached if first, scrabbling slightly as I almost threw it over my shoulder in my hurry to answer it before him. I would normally let Dad answer during the day, avoiding awkward conversations with foreign call centres and scams, Mum's request told me I should be the one to answer it.

"Hello?"

Dad was leaning against the doorframe, arms folded, some pink flushed in his cheeks. He wasn't a large man, but his presence filled the doorframe. Jeez, he could be scary if he wanted to be. Mum stood at the top of the stairs in her woolly, white dressing gown, a towel slung over her arm. This must be one important phone call.

"Marcus, it's Damien. Last night, it wasn't just the Michaels kid, yours was there too. O'Donnell almost caught her," I half turned away, turning my back on Dad as I listened intently, mentally noting down names.

Damien-?

Michaels- that's Cowan's surname

O'Donnell- that's our headmaster

Suddenly Dad was grabbing the back of my head, "Jesus Mel!" he exclaimed, "What happened to you head?" He prodded it with a thumb, pretty roughly, and I started smacking him with the phone, screaming "You're hurting, let go!" Next to my ear, a stream of swearwords erupted from the phone in my hand.

"What did you do last night?" he demanded. Then he caught sight of my bruised neck and things became somewhat chaotic.

"I fell out a tree!" I yelled desperately, which in my defence, was partially true. He finally let go and snatched the phone from my grasp, holding it to his ear, "I'm taking you to A&E, right now,"

"I'm fine!" I moaned, "Sleep, I just need sleep,"

Dad was ignoring me, murmuring into the phone with his back to me, "No, no, not now, I told you not to, no, just leave us alone," My head was throbbing and my

37

fingers danced lightly over the wound. The hallway was tilting and everything sounded like it was underwater again.

The next thing I knew the phone was back on the hook, and Dad was looking into my eyes, "You're pupils are dilated. How come Cowan didn't drive you to the hospital?" He was pushing me out the front door, towards the car. There was no time to ask about the phone call, or the reason for Dad's reaction.

"Rear windscreen was smashed,"

"What?"

"I shouldn't have told you that,"

He sighed, "Let's just get that wound checked out,"

Chapter 6

11:30… 11:31…. 11:32…..

The clock that hung on the clinically clean wall of the hospital seemed to be slowing down. Then again, I had thought that at nine o'clock when the minute hand took half an hour to move from the twelve to the one. I sat swinging my legs childishly on the bed. The events of the past day or so were vivid in my mind. I focused on small things, such as my laces, the guidelines painted on the floor, the clocks. We only had to wait an hour and a half, and after that the doctor had said it was a small cut, mostly bruising and swelling that would go down in a few days, the same was said for my neck. Dad was picking up some painkillers as I sat there. There was nothing dangerous at all about the graze. Dad had overreacted.

And I'm sure Dad would like me to admit that I also overreacted.

I think I reacted perfectly reasonably.

"What? What the hell? No! You can't tell me who I may and may not be friends with! Who gave you that control? You have no right! And after what has just happened, you expect me just to abandon him? Who are you? What- I can't even-"

"I'm just saying-"

"No, you don't get to 'just say'!"

"I'm thinking of your health! You've hit your head pretty nastily-"

"You're not listening!"

"-Only knows what happened to your neck, and you mentioned the rear windscreen getting smashed. I'm trying to keep you safe,"

"By simply cutting him out and going to Courtney's for dinner? What's he gonna think?"

"I'm only suggesting it," he pacified, slowly backing out of the door with his hands up in surrender, "I'll be right back with your medicine,"

That had been 17 minutes ago. There was no one else around; the room I was waiting in was empty of anything except a curtain, a sink, a bed, and some sort of monitor all looking as if they had been soaked in bleach to make them so blindingly white. Then there was myself, sticking out like a sore thumb. People were storming past the doorway, white coats flying, feet slapping on the linoleum. I felt awkward, as if I was preventing the treatment of someone who needed it by simply existing. As if I was a waste of space.

I was about to get up and search for Dad when a woman suddenly filled the doorway. It was Huang, tall and imposing, she looked like she must have originally been from Taiwan. I remembered her from Cass's funeral. She glanced me up and down before introducing herself, "I'm Lisa Huang," she said her accent relatively thick.

"Yeah, my Dad knows you?"

"I'm in charge here," she continued as if I hadn't said anything, "He asked me to speak to you about what happened last night,"

I took note of her formal clothing and heavily made up face, as if she really belonged on the set of a TV show rather than in a hospital. I only nodded, worried that I would blurt the wrong thing again. My head pounded as I tried to think of where I had seen her before.

She moved further into the room, her steps purposeful and intimidating, "He thinks that you won't tell him anything because you're scared of how he might react. Well, you can tell me,"

So that you can go to straight to him and tell him everything? I don't think so.

I half shrugged, "There's nothing to tell him that I haven't already said," I tried, speaking slowly and carefully. It didn't sound like my voice, more like the croak of a toad who hasn't spoken for a while, "I'm sorry, who are you again?"

She smiled gently, or at least tried to. A for effort. "There's a few things that still need explaining," She continued, ignoring my question completely.

"Like what?"

"You don't get bruises like that by falling out of a tree,"

Ah. Of course not. We both knew that I was stumped so I didn't say anything. I simply stared at her blank faced, wondering if there was any point in coming up with a lie.

"We need to know if someone hurt you Mel," Suddenly I understood why she was pushing so hard. Of course Dad was worried, he was my father. What had happened last night had twisted my idea of who I could trust. I'd been scared witless and still hadn't quite recovered my common sense, that was all. I could tell these people everything, and Dad would be able to sort all out.

I opened my mouth, ready to spill everything when the phone call came rushing back. That man, Damien, had phoned Dad, knowing that I had been there last night. That meant that Dad knew, so what was the point in hiding? Similarly, what was the point in telling? Dad knew I had been there. He was obviously a part of something, whether intentionally or not (I desperately hoped the latter) and I was getting sucked into it too. I decided there and then that I wouldn't. Stupidly, I believed that if I ignored it, it would go away.

You are so wrong.

I bit my tongue and didn't say anything.

Huang sighed, frustrated, "Perhaps we should try again another time?" she suggested, "When you're feeling better,"

I nodded and she offered to help me find Dad, which I accepted. I slipped off the bed and followed her, managing to make it to the doorway without falling over. I gripped the frame, allowing the dizziness to pass, before heading out into the chaos that was the corridor. It was difficult to follow Huang since doctors and nurses and administration staff hurtled past me in a blur on either sides, everything moving at 100mph. Perhaps it was me. I could feel the pad that was secured to the back of my head slipping uncomfortably but every time I went to adjust it, it hadn't moved.

We found Dad in the pharmacy, near the front of the hospital, chatting to none other than Howard Berkeley. Huang, after a curt nod at Dad, left. Berkeley appeared to have just exited the gift shop because he was holding a big bunch of ugly daisies and half-dead foxgloves. His sweaty face lit up as he saw me and the nausea returned with a sickening thump in the back of my throat. I was taller than him, and as I reached the pair, I was amused to see that I could look down on him.

He chuckled at something Dad said, his jowls wobbling worse than any jelly I'd seen, and then he turned to me and held the bunch of flowers out with a stiff, robotic arm. "For you," he rumbled, "I heard about your accident and decided I must come and show some comfort, especially after what has happened,"

I self-consciously took the pathetic bouquet. They drooped in my hand and it made me feel worse rather than better. Suddenly aware that I was receiving flowers from the mayor, I glanced around in search of a flashing camera or scribbling journalist. Berkeley noticed this and chuckled again, "Don't worry, no one knows I'm here. No paparazzi," He winked. Ugh.

"We were just discussing that invitation to dinner," Dad said cheerfully and I looked at him, my facing practically screaming 'Why are you friends with this sleezeball?!' "You've said yes, haven't you?"

Well I can hardly say no now, can I? "Are you sure it won't be too much trouble?" I asked politely instead, crushing the flowers in an attempt to stay calm, "I'd hate to be an inconvenience,"

"No, no, not at all," Berkeley waved away my concerns, "Your father and I, we are very close," he put a hand on Dad's shoulder and I supressed a smile as Dad winced, "He's told me how much you are struggling to come to terms with what's occurred and I could hardly allow my best friend's (another wince Dad?) daughter fall into the... ahem, wrong crowd,"

The crowd I'm with now is the crowd I've always been with. I almost screamed, but luckily I had the flowers to take the brute force of my anger, "Well yeah, it is hard," I admitted, awkwardly staring at my shoes, "But I don't doubt the support of my friends..." I faultered, "Friend,"

"Even when they put you in dangerous situations?" he asked, raising an eyebrow.

"Depends on what you consider a 'dangerous situation'," I joked. I gestured to my injury, "This, this was caused by me falling out of the tree in Cowan's back garden," I lied. It was a hell of a lot easier to lie to Berkeley than it was to Dad, they came out nice and smooth, "I'm not the most graceful, I get it from Dad," I stared at him meaningfully.

"We should probably get home," Dad interrupted, guiding me by the shoulders away from Berkeley, "For her rest,"

"I'll have to get back to you on that invitation," I called over my shoulder as Dad pushed me out the double doors, "I don't know if I'll be 100 percent,"

"She'll make it," Dad interjected.

"I'll confirm!"

Chapter 7

The car journey home probably could have gone better. Dad and I both took part in a screaming match which ended in one sore throat, tears, snot, and one thoroughly lost temper, all belonging to me. I retreated to my room as soon as I was over the threshold. I curled up under my duvet, trying to shut out the muffled sounds of Dad shouting down the phone. I could understand his need to protect me, but this, this sudden controlling of my life was intolerable.

I scrabbled for my phone off my bedside table and returned to the foetal position, hidden beneath my duvet. I winced as the phone screen blinded me momentarily and then managed a small laugh at the amount of messages Cowan had sent after my rather ominous message: Dad's taking me to A&E: 128 Facebook messages, 32 texts, 18 missed calls, and 68 snapchats. Jeez Cowan, do you have a life?

I messaged back a few words: I'm fine, just prescribed painkillers, need to talk ASAP.

That didn't make me feel as better as I had originally anticipated. The one person I really wanted to talk to was dead. Cass would have an answer to why this was happening, why Dad was changing, why I was being hunted by devil worshippers. Her answer wouldn't be particularly awe-inspiring. I could already hear her words in my head: "Fate," she'd say simply, "This is meant to happen because it's s'posed to teach you a lesson, you're s'posed to learn something,"

"What can I learn from this?" I whispered in response.

"Who knows?"

"Helpful Cass, real helpful,"

"I'd say you need to look deep inside yourself, but let's be honest, you never went for any of that crap,"

I sat up, throwing the duvet back and accidentally sending my phone flying across the room. It sounded as if Cass was standing right next to my bed, like she used to when she was fiddling with my lava lamp, watching the wax float lethargically up and down. I hadn't switched it on since she disappeared.

"Cass?"

Silence.

I was imagining it. I flicked the lava lamp on anyway.

My phone lit up, vibrating and moving across the floor in its excitement to tell me I had a message. I couldn't quite commit myself to leaving my bed and so, a few seconds later, I was reaching precariously across the floor with nothing but my feet still actually on the bed. I crawled back in my cocoon, cradling my phone and blocking out any thoughts of Cass.

The phone proudly announced the two messages, one from Cowan (naturally) and the other was from Courtney. Oh no.

'So, are you a clairvoyant?'

'Hardly,'

'Do you see into the future?'

'Not really,'

'Cass, you are so not helping yourself,'

'You're such an attention seeker! No one pays you enough of it, so you, like, make up lies so people talk to you? How childish! Can I tell you something though? No offence, it's not working. People talk about you and they say, well, like, nasty things,'

I could feel Cass's hand in mine as I dragged her away...

Suddenly, my phone flickered back into focus and I was wrapped up in my duvet again, no longer in the corridor at school. With Cass. I curled up in a ball, trying to drown the memories. When it came to people, I was usually optimistic. I was convinced that there was some sort of good in everyone. But when it came to Courtney Berkeley with her taunts, digs, and spiteful 'no offences', there was no good in her. "Her yin yang was all black" Cass would say. I was crying again, and my throat hurt.

It took me a while to unlock my phone. When I did, I flexed my hand and then read the message:

'Hey. Dad just said your staying for dinner? Sorry about wht happened I'll be glad if you could make it dinner would be nice XD Cx'

Well, that could have been worse. Perhaps the face was slightly inappropriate. Ignoring the casual ignorance for grammatical laws, I responded with a quick Thanks, dinner would be great, sent it and then panicked about times and dress code and so that message was followed by three sloppy messages, asking for details.

After a few seconds, Cowan phoned offering to pick me up but I think I shocked him by hissing down the phone, "Don't come to the house! I'll meet you at the Green,"

I think I was sick of lying in bed: of staring at the pink glowing underside of the duvet, of wiping condensation off the phone screen, of blocking memories. Cass's voice kept wriggling back into my mind, telling me to go to places, to talk to these certain people, to do this and do that.

"I can do my own thing!"

I think getting out of the house would do me good.

Sneaking past Dad turned out to be easy. He had sunken into his favourite past time of eating pop tarts in front of TV. Ah, guilty pleasures. I managed to slip out of the front door, cradling the last packet of pop tarts that heaway from Cass
 had carelessly left on the kitchen counter.

The Green wasn't far from my house. It made up the back of the highschool. It was wide expanse of (believe it or not) green grass, rolling down at the far end so it seamlessly flowed into the oaks and ash and pines of Raven's Wood. It was so much more beautiful this side, fuller almost, twice as alive as it was by the church. If you sat on the climbing frame, with you back to the school that was a blight on the landscape, and watched the sun fall behind the leaves, for just a moment it was a spot of unforgettable, serene beauty.

It was our spot.

I ran all the way, taking a childish pleasure in the way the wind swept past me, through my hair, through my mind, clearing it of the cloudy thoughts that were slowly becoming thunderous. Just for those few seconds. Cowan was already there when I arrived, legs dangling over the edge below the monkey bars, facing west. I clambered up to join him, a pop tart already in my mouth.

"Waddup," I mumbled through pastry and sugar, still gasping for breath.

"Why can't I come to your house?" Straight to the point.

"Dat's what ah need do 'alk do oo bout,"

"Okay, finish what you're eating and then talk to me,"

I chewed for a minute, watching the leaves get swept up in the breeze, and then quickly explained what had happened at the hospital. It didn't take me long and I was glad that Cowan found my description of Berkeley just as funny as I did.

"So, you're not allowed to be friends with me anymore?" he asked once I finished. He nibbled around the icing of his pop tart.

"That about sums it up,"

"And the fact that you have to go to Courtney's is a more pressing matter than the fact that we could possibly be being stalked by devil worshippers?"

I paused for a moment, feigning thought, "I believe so,"

"Talk about priorities,"

"I've been trying to not think about what happened last night," I mumbled, absent-mindedly rubbing my throat.

Cowan looked at me with disbelief and I couldn't understand why. Surely it was natural not to want to contemplate such a traumatic event? Why was that so unfathomable to him?

"But what happened was so important,"

"Oh, I bet it was important!" I snapped, "Had you actually explained to me what you saw,"

"Maybe if you hadn't been such a coward you would have seen it with me,"

It was my turn to stare at him in disbelief, "What is wrong with you?"

"You just don't seem to be focusing on the matters that need focusing on," his voice swelled for a moment before he recovered his composure and continued, "Seriously, I don't think you should go to Courtney's. If I'm honest, I don't think there's any point,"

"Why do you say that?"

He fiddled with the pastry of his pop tart for a minute, pulling it apart flake by flake, avoiding the question. The setting sun was shining directly in our faces and it lit up his cheeks and his hair and his eyelashes and he was bathed in this golden glow. My heart fluttered stupidly and I looked away, waiting for his answer. It took him a long time and I suddenly felt awkward and I didn't want to interrupt the sudden tension between us. I didn't even know what tension it was or how I was supposed to react to it so I stuffed another pop tart into my mouth and stared steadfastly at the trees.

Eventually he murmured, "I don't think she'll be there. I'm… I'm scared Mel," he smiled weakly, "That's all there is to it. I'm not only scared for myself, but I'm scared for you now, especially. See, I thought I saw her, Courtney of all people, last night. She was, you know, lying on this stone dais and I swear she wasn't… moving. And now all of a sudden you're invited to their house for dinner? I can't let you be in danger, for you to go the same way as Cass did,"

"You think they had something to do with Cass?"

"Isn't that what you think?"

I didn't move my gaze away from the edge of the forest. This was the reason I hadn't wanted to think about those people because every single train of thought led to that inevitable conclusion. Why else had she vanished like she had? Found the way she was? There was no doubt that she wasn't dead now either, not anymore, not after what I'd seen. The last bit of hope I had been clinging onto had been wiped out. It hit me again like a steam train. Cass was never coming back.

Yet, I knew that there was a small part of me, right at the back of my mind, that stubbornly argued: She's still here.

I inhaled shakily, trying hard not to cry again. That's all I seemed capable of doing when I thought about Cass.

When I finally got control, I steered the conversation away from Cass, "You've got to have it wrong," I said, "Courtney messaged me today about dinner tomorrow. She seemed very much alive," You can't always be sure of that though, can you? "I'm going Cowan," I decided, "After what you've told me, maybe I can see what I can find at their house?"

"No, I can't let you do that, not on your own," I finally met his gaze and saw how scared he truly was. Scared of someone else getting hurt and knowing that he could have stopped it.

"What's the worst that can happen?" I asked, smiling slightly, "I'll call you right away if Courtney turns out to be a zombie okay?"

He shook his head in exasperation, but he was smiling too. The sun was finally dropping behind the trees, and its golden glow deepened to an orange before fading to purple and blue. It was glorious or it would have been had this gigantic nightmare not been hanging over us, twisting everything I thought I believed in into an unrecognisable tangle of hope and fear and death. "Promise you'll be careful and that you'll message me if anything goes wrong,"

"Would I do anything else?"

We jumped down and left when the light faded and mysterious shadows started to gather at the edges of the trees.

Chapter 8

The weather was completely different from yesterday. Despite the wonderful sunset that Cowan and I had watched (after which he drove me home whilst proudly pointing out his new rear windscreen) heavy clouds, as black as my brooding mood, had rolled in and released Niagara Falls. It hadn't stopped raining for shy on twelve hours.

The rain, despite having lasted so long, was still falling heavily. It bounced off the bonnet of the car and drummed loudly on the roof, creating multiple races down the windows. The windscreen wipers were throwing themselves back and forth across the window in a vain attempt to keep it clear of the relentless water. I was reminded of Leanne's face at the funeral.

I stayed in the passenger seat, clutching my sweaty hands together partly in nerves and partly to stop me from prodding the cut on the back of my head. I had removed the pad in the shower this morning and it already looked much better, but I could still feel it throbbing. I'd braided my hair in a plait around my head to hide it but it made me feel young and childish. I didn't belong with these people. They were worlds apart from what I was used to. I wasn't just scared of the fact that Courtney could possibly be dead, or that somebody had tried to kill her, I was also utterly terrified of having to sit down with a family I despised and have a decent conversation with them.

I adjusted the scarf around my neck.

"This is it kiddo, time for you to get out,"

"But it's raining,"

"You think that's going to stop me from kicking you out of this car?"

I laughed drily, "Of course not. I'll see you on the otherside,"

"You'll be fine,"

"Huh,"

"Love you kiddo,"

I nodded, took a deep breath and counted to three before leaping out of the car and hurtling towards the porch. I could barely make out any of the house in the driving rain. All I could sense was its sheer size as it loomed over me out of the darkness. I knew it was a huge building, consisting of soaring columns and balconies with black painted metal rails, cute little flowers in window boxes and windows upon windows the size of doors. I caught sight of only one singularly lit room where the light flickered rhythmically. I felt a wave of nausea as I dived under shelter, pushing the thoughts of flickering flames aside.

Dad gave me a thumbs up from the car and I had to resist the urge to throw a middle finger back at him. I rang the doorbell, nervously gripping the bottle of wine that he had whipped out from the back of the garage. The door was answered by a tall man, his hair slicked so severely back that it seemed to take the skin with it, stretching out over the high cheekbones and pulling his mouth into a permanent grimace.

I gulped.

A thin eyebrow travelled up the wide expanse of forehead, "Can I be of service?"

"Uh, hi," I whispered. I held the bottle out awkwardly, "Mr Berkeley invited me for dinner?"

"Ah, you're Miss Parker?"

"Yup,"

He beckoned me in, and I followed him through the hall that was lined with tables upon which stood a phenomenal amount of trophies and medals and certificates. Pictures of the Courtney in various sporting competitions were framed next to the corresponding award. I didn't belong here, I thought. I don't even like sport.

The man, who I assumed to be the Butler, had disappeared into a side door and I stood there feeling terribly awkward whilst clutching the bottle. I tried not to look around the room in awe. It was huge. What I could see of the wallpaper beneath the dozens of gilded frames was expensive and luxurious curtains trailed on the endless black and white marble squares that made up the hallway floor. It left me feeling like an expendable pawn in a vast chessboard. Each door was made of a rich mahogany that reflected the glittering chandeliers and the stairway seemed straight from the Titanic: all plush carpets and solid wood.

It was as I was admiring/being disgusted at the ridiculous and sheer amount of wealth this family could waste when I saw her again. The back of my head began to sting. She was standing at the top of the staircase and even at this distance, I could see her muddied leggings and badges flashing in the artificial light.

I froze.

Her face was just as expressionless as it had been the last time I saw her. She was so pale, she was translucent and her freckles stood out as dark, angry spots. Her empty eyes were staring at me and now they were slowly moving over the banisters towards a door at the far end of the landing. Her head tilted lethargically to the side. She pointed at the door. Her vacant gaze turned back to me. And then she lifted her chin and for the first time, I saw the gash.

"Cass?" I whined, "Please,"

Three doors flew open simultaneously.
I dropped the bottle.

Chapter 9

"I am so sorry,"

I had to meet the gaze of four startled people: the butler had returned with squat Mr Berkeley; Blake, who I was convinced was perpetually high, had slouched through another door on the ground floor; Courtney, who was staring at me with poorly disguised contempt, had emerged from the door that Cass had been pointing at. I was almost disappointed to see that she was alive.

Cass had vanished. I was standing in a pool of red wine that was soaking into my white converse and it looked like I had just had a terrible accident. Courtney had gone almost as pale as Cass had been and Blake simply looked slightly perturbed as if he wasn't entirely sure why I was standing in a pool of red liquid in his hall. There was silence before he said, "Carrie, is that you?"

I snorted nervously and tried to keep the wobble out of my voice, "I won't go on a psycho trip and kill everyone, I swear," Carrie was one of Cass's favourite films, she made me watch the original and all the various remakes.

Mr Berkeley bustled over and danced around the edges of the puddle before saying, "Come along Jason, help her out please. Don't worry my dear, accidents happen," he twittered. His pointless dithering put me in mind of a fragile and somewhat deranged bird.

The butler, now named Jason, retreated again to fetch something to clean up the mess. Blake hadn't moved (he was just swaying on the spot and staring at an apparently interesting area of wall at the top of the stairs) but Courtney leapt into action, barrelling along the landing and bounding down the stairs, stopping daintily on the bottom step.

"Melanie! You sure know how to make an entrance!" she burbled. Her father smiled, nodded twice and dragged his son out of the room. I was left alone with Courtney and my puddle.

"I am genuinely so sorry about this. You all came in at once, it made me jump," I lied.

Courtney tilted her head to the side, her face had an expression of perfect innocence plastered on. "I'm so glad you came," she said instead and smiled but it was a little forced. She obviously didn't like me, so why was I here? "I thought you were the best person to talk to about this and since our Dads are such close friends, I thought 'Dinner!'"

Wow, you can actually think?

"People are always so much more agreeable after they've eaten, you know?"

I nodded, only half understanding. It seemed strange that she would use the word 'agreeable', as if I wasn't agreeable already. And what exactly did she want to talk about?

We lapsed into silence and she stared hard at me, her head still tilted to the side like a confused puppy dog as if she wasn't entirely sure why I was there either.

"I'm sorry about the wine," I apologised again, scrabbling for some way to break the silence.

"You don't need to worry about that,"

Silence.

"I didn't realise how big your house was on the inside. It doesn't seem like that on the outside," That was a complete and utter lie, "Kinda like the Tardis, huh?"

"Mmm,"

I frowned at her, struggling, and was about to ask some inane question about her schoolwork or something equally boring when Blake drifted back into the hall carrying a jug of water, followed by Jason. The butler was carrying several roles of kitchen role and the next few minutes were filled with mumbled apologies, awkward dancing to avoid spilt wine, and half a dozen disdainful and superior glances from Courtney.

Jason retreated again and I was left with sodden, stained shoes and the Berkeley siblings. Blake was staring into space again and Courtney sighed and, flinging her hair over her shoulder, said, "We have so many really interesting things to chat about, you know? Like, about what's happened, about-" she pauses, "Cass,"

Oh, so that's why I'm here. For 'The Gossip'.

Blake snorted, and I felt my stomach lurch in anger. What did she know about Cass? "If I remember right, you two weren't bezzies exactly,"

Courtney waved her hand, "You don't understand, that was banter!"

'Look at her! Who does she think she is?'

'If your eyeliner was any thicker, people are gonna think it's Halloween,'

'I've seen less rolls in a bakery,

You call that banter?

"Are you aware of the definition of 'banter'?" Blake somehow managed to drag his attention away from the fascinating speck of dust that existed on the landing.

Courtney tutted, flicked her hair, tutted again as she realised she was in the wrong and mirroring her father's sparrow-like movements said, "It's important that I talk to you about her. You and Cowan were closest to her right? So I figured you two would probably be able to make sense of my... issue," she glanced shiftily at her brother but he was already drifting out of the room towards the aroma of a roast dinner.

She wasn't getting away with it that easily, "But why the sudden interest in Cass?" I asked, tilting my head ever so slightly in mockery, "What's your 'issue'?"

I thought I caught a shadow passing over her face. Again, it was paired with a surreptitious glance about the hall, "I'll explain later," she said quietly.

A bell tinkled in the depth of the house, indicating that dinner was about to be served. Courtney waved and I followed. As we passed through the doorway to the dining room, a figure materialised out of the shadows. I flinched as stained fingers gripped my forearm.

"Did you see her?" Blake hissed and I swallowed the scream that had bubbled up in my throat.

"What the hell Blake?" His nails were beginning to dig in and my whole body was poised for instinctive flight, including my bladder.

"Did you?" he repeated.

"Who?" I played stupid. No way could we have seen the same thing.

"You did, didn't you?" he grinned, a sandy curl looped over one eye, "You saw her?"

"Blake, I..." am a terrible liar.

"Whatever you do, don't listen to Courtney. She may be my sister, but I don't trust her a bit,"

I paused, my hand hovering over the door handle, my mouth half open as I debated whether to admit or deny seeing Cass, "Okay Blake," I settled on, "I won't,"

That seemed to be enough for him and I followed him to the dining room.

"Would you like some gravy, dear?"

Ugh. "Yes please. I can't stand mash without a bit of gravy. It's just not worth eating, you know? Too dry and um... yeah," I trailed off, internally begging myself to stop talking. All four of them were staring at me as if I originated from Mars and had orange skin. Although that would hardly have been fair, they couldn't judge me even if I did have orange skin, Mrs Berkeley looked like a cheese puff with all that fake tan!

I took a deep breath, telling myself to calm down.

Dinner was a terribly awkward affair.

Mr Berkeley didn't shut up about the 'terrible incident' that was Cass. He rabbited on about the possible reasons behind her disappearance. "I've spoken to the police in relation to her disappearance you know," he was saying at one point. Dinner was nearly over, the plates almost empty. I was pushing my mash potatoes around the pool of gravy and was reminded of the pool of wine I had had to stand in. My shoes were dry now, but probably stained for good.

"The police have told me, in confidence of course," he continued, pointing his fork at Courtney in particular, "But they say it was mostly her own fault. Met someone on the internet, went to meet him, you know the story. Of course, there was nothing anyone could do about it, after she left,"

A carrot flew of Blake's plate, sending gravy splattering across the white table cloth. My knuckles were white because I was clutching my cutlery so hard. Mrs Berkeley was only nodding in agreement as she daintily sliced her meat into wafer thin pieces. Did they remember I was here?

They must have because Berkeley was staring right at me. I met his gaze with my own made of steel, daring him to go on. Of course, the idiot did, "Yes. Nobody could have done anything. Girls like that, girls who struggle to fit in, often try to fit in with someone online you know.

Psychologically proven, I'm told. They just look for acceptance,"

I didn't need acceptance. I had you guys! I was happy with who I was!

I swallowed down bile and laid my cutlery down, swaying slightly.

I looked away from Berkeley, glancing at Courtney who was glaring icily at her father and then at Blake who was staring at his plate, his hands shaking.

And still Berkeley carried on, "Did you know Carol, that acceptance is one of the most important things to a teenager?"

C'mon, why are you two listening to this crap?

"That sense of belonging, of fitting in, is vital for their growth,"

He's chatting bull!

"For them to grow into a fully functioning adult, they must fit into the school hierarchy,"

"Oh shut up you stupid little man!" My stomach dropped.

Cass hadn't said that last one. I had.

I was standing, my chair thrown back, heart pounding, breath quick and fast. I felt like I'd just outrun some devil-worshippers with an axe.

Oh no wait.

Berkeley was on his feet as well and our furious glares, could have created a conduit of fire between us. He was turning a bright red, and I watched as he slowly transformed into an angry tomato on top of a potato. He belonged on the dinner plate, not in real life.

He was opening his mouth when suddenly: "Oh my Gosh Mel," Courtney interjected loudly. She had diverted our attention enough for the tension between us to disperse somewhat. "I like, love your scarf. Although, y'know, I have a scarf that would match that dress a lot more than that one. Why don't we excuse ourselves and go upstairs?"

"I'd love to," I growled and followed her out of the room, throwing my fancy napkin into my plate so that it began to soak up the gravy. Berkeley had collapsed heavily into his chair, dabbing his sweating brow.

Courtney led me up the grand staircase in the hall and into her room. Her room made me cringe. It was tastefully designed with turquoise and cream walls, pine furniture and matching duvets and pillows. The only problems were the mess: empty pizza boxes littered the floor, dishes were piled on the bedside table, clothes were strewn across the floor, jewellery hung off door handles and mirrors and masses amount of makeup marked the walls, the carpet, and the central mirror; and the oddly, yet strategically placed glass unicorns, scented candles, and incense. I felt like I had just walked into the aftermath of an exploded teenager who hadn't quite grown out of her fairy tale childhood phase. I tried not to choke on the suffocating mixture of lavender and rotting food.

"I'll get straight to the point," Courtney said, sitting gracefully into a chair that was piled high with cardigans a moment before, "I want to talk about Cass," All false fronts had dropped away and Courtney's face was serious and interrogative.

I was kind of glad that Courtney wasn't pretending anymore, it meant I didn't need to either and I didn't need to find her hidden motive, "Oh so you haven't got a better matching scarf?" I asked, faking sadness.

"I know things," she puffed herself up with self-importance and ignoring me completely, continued "Because of Dad and his loose mouth. I know that you and Cowan went out the other night, at the church and you were seen running. Why?"

You wanna know why they were seen running? Because we were being chased.

I remained silent, not entirely sure where she was going with this. If Berkeley knew that Cowan and I had been there then that meant he was there, or someone he knew was. If Cowan was to be believed, Courtney had also been there too. Blake's words came back to me, "She may be my sister, but I don't trust her a bit,"

"And I know something else too..." she left the sentence hanging, as if she was trying to hook me like a fish and despite the fact that she was clumsy and I knew exactly what she was doing, I couldn't help but bite.

"Oh yeah? What's that?" I tried to keep my voice calm, burying my curiosity and desperation beneath casualness.

"They know about Cowan,"

I stared at her blankly. Who do? What do they know about Cowan? I think she was deliberately being vague in order to increase the tension and drama, a technique I had heard her use a thousand times in school. Similar to how I was now, her listeners would be trapped by her words, unable to do anything but wait for her to explain because they wouldn't want to come across as dumb or short-sighted. I was far too impatient to play her stupid little game.

"You're gonna have to elaborate," I smiled cheerily, knowing that it was the response that she was least expecting, "You're not making any sense Courtney,"

She sighed, flicked her hair over her shoulder in annoyance, "There are rumours. A lot of rumours and they're all saying the same thing. That Cass is coming back as a ghost and Cowan is the one seeing her,"

...

Crap.

I opened and closed my mouth a few times, mimicking a goldfish, truly shocked and trapped in Courtney's web. "How did you- Who said? How many people..." I stuttered, then, "Oh," as reality finally sunk in, "Oh crap," My knees weakened and they shook so much that I had to lean against the door in order to stay upright. I could have sworn that a look of triumph crossed Courtney's face but it was replaced by concern to so quickly that I couldn't be sure.

"I'm guessing these rumours are true?" she asked quietly.

I took a deep breath before managing a weak but determined, "Explain,"

Courtney's face contorted into a mask of anger, a mask that I had never seen before, one reserved for (I assumed) the people she loathed the most. I was quite proud that I made the privileged list. The look was gone in a few seconds and her features softened. I was impressed that her face could pass through so many expressions and not leave a trace. I wondered why my demand had made her so angry. She remained quiet for a moment longer, thoughtfully wrapping a piece of dyed hair around her finger before eventually saying, "There are these people, dangerous people. I know it sounds mad, but these people believe in the Devil: they like, follow him, and worship him, and they sacrifice for him. And these people have a lot of influence, they are in high places throughout the town so they can keep the stories of missing kids turning up brutally murdered quiet,"

I took note of her use of the plural for 'kids'.

"What are you saying?" I whispered.

"They murder these people for 'communicating'," she made sarcastic bunny ears with her fingers, "That means they speak to ghosts. I'm sure these people killed Cass. She always made such a big deal about it and then suddenly they find out that one of her best friends is communicating with her? That could cause a whole heap of trouble for them,"

"But ghosts don't exist Courtney," my mind was in turmoil, an uncontrollable mess of tumbling thoughts and conclusions that I couldn't comprehend because they were just too terrifying.

"Neither does the devil!" she shot back, "You think small things like whether the ghost of Cass is real is going to bother them?" She had this combination of smugness and disbelief on her face, like she knew she was the cleverest one in here and couldn't believe that no one else could get it.

I held my hands up in surrender, "Okay okay," my whole body was shaking so I slid to the floor and tried to stop the room from swaying. This information was overwhelming, my head was pounding and I had a hundred questions. I just needed time to order my thoughts.

I made a mental picture on the carpet, ignoring my throbbing head. I had this new group of people, apparent devil worshippers, who killed Cass. It seemed reasonable to assume that these were the same people that Cowan and I saw in the woods and who chased us with an axe. I mean, I hardly expect there to be two psychotic and deluded groups who worship Lucifer. What Courtney had told me confirmed the suspicions of Cowan and I, they were devil worshippers and they did kill teenagers.

Now, these Worshippers knew about Cowan and his communication with Cass. Awfully, I felt a tiny glimmer of relief. They didn't seem to know about me despite my experiences being more intense than Cowan's. My stomach tied itself into vicious knots at the idea that Cowan could be in danger. Courtney didn't know if it was true or not, although I was still wary of how she knew this information. I remembered the dig she had made about Berkeley and his loose mouth, and the idea that he might have been there too. I glanced at her and she was tapping away on her phone, barely noticing that I was still there. She seemed completely unperturbed by the fact her father could have connections with Devil Worshippers.

A question escaped before I could stop it, "Why are you telling me this? Why not tell Cowan directly?"

She honoured me with a raised eyebrow and a short, "Because he doesn't trust me, does he?"

I don't trust you either. "Why do you think that?" I pushed.

All her interest in me had gone, there was something way more fascinating on her phone screen now. She held a finger up, telling me to wait and I had the overwhelming urge to snatch her phone and throw it out the window. Finally, she found the time to speak to me, "He says he saw me when you were at the church. Obviously, I wasn't there but there's nothing I can do if I appear in his fantasies,"

My stomach twisted again, but this time in anger. What Cowan saw wasn't a fantasy! I trusted him and therefore believed him when he assured me it was real. Courtney made it sound delusional and fake, so dirty and wrong.

"Who told you that?" I demanded. I hadn't actually admitted to being at the church yet, but there didn't seem any point denying it either. I could feel my temper intensifying, as if it was a rubber band and someone was stretching it to breaking point.

"I've been messaging Cowan, seems like he's finally opening up a bit. Well, now that you're here anyway,"

The rubber band snapped.

Cowan had told Courtney about the church? Could he genuinely be that stupid? Or was he too blinded by her fake but beautiful looks? If I didn't leave within the next five minutes, the murdered teenage count was going to increase by one.

"Look, see?" she waved the phone in my face and all I caught was the bright pink of the heart emojis. That was the last straw.

"I'm leaving,"

Courtney blinked, confused, "Why?"

"You're talking to Cowan now, it's obvious that you don't need me anymore," Suddenly, someone else was sitting beside me. I didn't need to look directly to see it was Cass. I could make out her ripped and muddied stripy leggings in my peripheral vision. I didn't want to look, I didn't want to see her neck again.

I opened the door and stumbled through to get away from Cass now as well as Courtney. All the injuries I had sustained were playing up again, sending waves of pain around my skull. I had managed to reach the front door before Courtney bothered to follow me. She stood at the top of the landing and Cass stood close behind her, like a reverse guardian angel. Cass was more likely to guide Courtney to hell than heaven.

"You can't go now," even when she whined, Courtney's voice was still perfectly harmonious, "We still have so much to talk about,"

"What? What could we possibly talk about that you can't already chat about to Cowan?" I demanded, my fury getting the better of me.

Even Courtney's temper was beginning to fray like an old, ugly rug, "Oh I don't know, how about the fact that Cowan isn't the only one who can talk to Cass?" she responded sarcastically, flipping her hair over her shoulder.

If she wants it to stay there, she should invest in a headband.

"Shut up Cass!" There was silence as I realised my mistake. At least Cass had the decency to look sheepish. I corrected myself, "Courtney,"

"Goodbye Melanie,"

I glared at her one last time, my chest contracting in panic, and slammed the door as hard as I could on the way out. It didn't occur to me then how childish my actions had been or quite how serious a mistake I had made. As I stormed away down the street, the rain washed me away.

Chapter 10

I was so cold.

I didn't think it was that far to my house, but the distance seemed to have elongated in the heavy rain. My hair was plastered to my forehead, my clothes clinging to me like a second skin. I couldn't feel my toes and fingers were so numb that I hadn't realised that I had let go of my scarf. I didn't know where I had lost it. I didn't even know where I had lost my resolve and possibly my sanity either. That could also be on the road somewhere, or tangled in a hedge. Maybe Cowan would see it, and pick it up for me.

Unfortunately, Cass hadn't lost her resolve. She hadn't given up. That was like her. Through the driving rain, I could see her shadowy outline because the droplets were bouncing off her shoulders too. I didn't know why it had taken me until now, but I finally believed her. Or at least, believed that ghosts could exist. She had given me enough credible evidence.

"Lovely weather we're having," I called to her. She didn't reply, just turned her head away.

"I've seen better," the voice hurled me back to reality with a fearful jolt. I turned, half expecting a figure in a cloak wielding an axe. But no, it was Blake, his hair dripping and a fag drooping sadly from between his lips.

"Is that even lit?" I asked, gesturing to it.

He shook his head, looking almost as sad as it, "It went out and I forgot a lighter. Don't s'pose you…?"

"No. Y'know, smoking's bad for you,"

Blake sighed, "So are a lot of other things,"

We both stared down the road. Everything was drenched in the dark blue of the night and there was an almost imperceptible fine line between the broiling clouds and ground at the horizon. Cass's outline had paused with her hands on her hips. I glanced at Blake and on his face was an expression of such heartache and longing that I felt I was invading his personal space by just looking at him. I backed away, thinking about Cowan and wondering if he had ever looked at me like that or whether it had always been Cass.

Blake wiped his nose and grinned, "Maybe we should get out of the rain?"

I laughed awkwardly, "Yeah, I think that's a good idea,"

The road we were standing on was lined with hedges, but the hedges were punctuated every now and then with yew trees or chestnuts. We hurried to the nearest one, despite the fact that the rain itself was finally starting to let off, becoming a light drizzle. My breath fogged in the evening air as we stood together and a sense of serenity swept over me. I stared upwards. The great branches had successfully shielded the ground from the downpour so that it crackled underfoot. Each bough crisscrossed with several others, intersecting, meeting and connecting, creating a secret, dim world in the darkness. It had stopped raining and everything around the tree seemed to be slowly unfurling, opening up to the clearing night sky, like it was an alternative, darker Spring. It smelt beautiful, of leaves and grass and dirt.

"You can see her, can't you? Please tell me I'm not mad," Blake was scuffing his shoe in the dirt like a small boy who just got caught stealing cookies.

For a moment, I hesitated. The only reason Courtney had invited me to dinner was to get information about Cowan and about Cass. How could I be sure that Blake wasn't doing the same? I met his gaze and I couldn't find any alternative motive except the need to know that he wasn't alone.

"Yeah, I can,"

"Cowan too?"

"Yeah, not as much though,"

He nodded, as if it was what he expected, "It's her but it's not,"

I looked at Cass. She had come forward, outlined in the moonlight, her make-up stark against her white face. Blake was right, it was her. It was her style, her ginger frizzy hair, it was physically Cass. Yet it wasn't: the empty, expressionless face, the slit throat. All the things that made Cass who she was were missing. It made me feel as I was missing something too.

"Why us?" I asked, hugging myself to keep the cold out. I pulled my phone out, quickly messaging Dad to come pick me up before tucking it back in my pocket. Blake still hadn't answered by the time I'd done that, and it was a few more minutes before he finally said something.

"She must want our help,"

"To do what?"

"To stop these people," his breath fogged in the air, billowing outwards in a cloud before dispersing so that it seemed like it never existed, only to be replaced again by another so that the old one wouldn't be forgotten.

"You believe that too?"

Blake sighed and I couldn't help but see Courtney reflected in him. They had the same stature, tall and skinny, although Blake slouched more. Blake had Courtney's eyes and Courtney had Blake's nose. It was almost funny that two people could look so similar yet be so different.

"How can I not?" he laughed softly and dug his hands into his pockets, "We've all seen them, we seen what they've done. It's not like I can pretend they don't exist because I'm scared of them,"

I looked sheepishly at my feet and felt my cheeks burn. That's exactly what I had been trying to do. For the first time, I looked at Blake and saw him not as that weird kid who sat at the back of the class and stared into space, but as a brave and determined man who cared for Cass above anything else.

Then I realised, "You two? You were…?"

He nodded, "I thought you knew?"

I shook my head, my mouth still hanging open at the revelation. We both looked for Cass but she had vanished. Of course. I scrabbled for something to say. I wanted to tell him how happy I was for the two of them because I genuinely was, but then I remembered that Cass was dead and there wasn't a lot to be happy about anymore.

I said I was happy for him anyway, despite it being pointless, and it made him smile which warmed me from the inside. For a moment, I couldn't feel the cold or the pain. I could just feel the warm little ball of happiness in my chest for Cass and Blake and I focused on it and tried to get it to grow but it was snuffed out violently by a gust of wind called 'reality'.

"We'll have to do something," Blake said with resolve, "So that she can, y'know, move on,"

I nodded in agreement, fighting the cold that was seeping back into my limbs. "Do we just need to expose them or what?"

Blake's voice was low and quiet when he next spoke, and it was laced with menace, "We need to take them down," He fell into silence and I shifted awkwardly, not quite sharing his grim determination. The rain had lightened off and was now falling in a thin drizzle, creating quiet pitter-pats on the leaves above our heads.

Blake interrupted their continuous, rhythmic sound, "There's something else,"

"What?"

"Well," he searched for the right words, the cigarette glowing dejectedly in his trembling fingers, "I found something. Something you should know about,"

I stared up at him, through the strands of damp hair that had been plastered to my forehead by the rain, "What's that?" Our voices had sunk into whispers despite the fact that we were in the middle of nowhere in the dead of night. Who could possibly be out here listening?

Two headlights suddenly lit up the entire road and Blake's face was as white as Cass's had been but less lost and more serious and resolute. My heart leapt into rapid racing and I knew that we would run out of time, "What is it Blake?"

Blake's face had melted from his mask of determination to an expression probably similar to mine: panic. He stuttered, sucked one last drag and muttered, "I'll tell you later, it can wait,"

"Blake no," I winced in the artificial light. It was so bright that it seemed to burn behind my eyes. I had to hold a hand up and squint to see the licence plate. The lights were flicked off and someone got out of the car but I couldn't quite make out who it was, the lights had dazzled me and I was still seeing spots.

"Mel?"

"Dad?" I blinked a few times and finally got my night vision back. He had a hood pulled over his head and I had uncomfortable images of the Worshippers flashing in my mind.

"What the Devil are you doing all the way out here?" he demanded.

I looked at Blake, hoping that he would answer but he'd conveniently found something fascinating in the dirt and had pretended not to hear. I shrugged, one of his pet hates, "I have no answer to that," I said simply, "We went for a walk and got caught in the rain,"

"Just get in the car, the pair of you," I did as I was told, and Blake awkwardly got into the backseat. He had crumpled up his soggy cigarette and stuffed it into his jeans pocket, as if he wanted to make a good impression on Dad.

As if hanging out with his only daughter in the middle of the night could possibly make a bad one.

I slid into the passenger seat and Blake collapsed into the back. I glared at him in the wing mirror, annoyed that he had stopped talking so easily at the first sight of danger. He didn't meet my eyes as he mumbled an apology to Dad.

Dad shrugged it off.

Hypocrite.

"Whatever Blake. You should have known better, that's all," he said, flicking the ignition on, "You've got to be careful, you don't know who's out there these days-"

Then the front of the car exploded. I screamed, irrationally convinced that it was ploy from the Worshippers to kill us. Blake yelled and Dad bellowed louder than the pair of us put together, gripping the steering wheel as if it was the only buoyancy life ring left in a sinking boat.

We saw the extent of the damage when Dad flicked his torch and overhead lights on. There were two shallow dents in the metal, small, almost hand-sized. I stared at them disbelieving, grasping what had really happened. I glanced around desperately, looking for her, whilst Blake said, trying to cover up the shaking in his voice, "Was that the engine?"

But Dad wasn't even looking at the bonnet anymore. He was training the torch beam slowly across the hedge that separated the road from the fields. "Dad?"

"No kiddo, it wasn't the engine,"

The beam shuddered to a stop and I thought he had caught her but there was nothing in the spotlight except the drizzling rain. A slight movement to the left. Dad had stopped purposefully before he hit her, so that her outline was clear in the darkness. She was staring at me, shaking her head vigorously, like she used to when I was being particularly slow or stupid or had just made a really bad decision.

Then she stared directly at Dad and flipped him the middle finger. Blake swore and I gaped.

Classic Cass.

"Can we go home now Dad? Please?" I whined, "I want to go home,"

Dad didn't respond. He just clicked off the torch, threw it into the backseat with probably more fury than he intended, and twisted the key with one, vicious motion. Blake flinched as the torch bounced off the seat next to him. Dad threw the car into reverse, barrelled across the road and then careened onto the lane. I was beginning to doubt that it wasn't only the two of us who could see Cass.

Chapter 11

I thought, when I clambered into bed, that I would submit to the cliché of 'falling asleep as soon as my head hit the pillow' but unfortunately this wasn't the case. I spent the night tossing and turning, struggling to get comfortable because something was always aching or hurting or had pins and needles. I managed to establish at ten past two that I wasn't going to get to sleep until I discovered what Blake had wanted to tell me.

In the darkness, I groped for my phone that I was sure I had left on the bedstand. After knocking over some body spray and make up on to the floor, I remembered that my phone was still residing in my jeans and so after rummaging through them, I finally found it stuck on silent. That explained why I hadn't known that Cowan had spammed my phone again.

Flicking on my phone, I winced at the brightness but managed to type out a message to Cowan, telling him that we needed to talk whilst casually ignoring his messages that got gradually angrier and angrier. It was usually Cass who wound Cowan up, and it didn't take her long to get him red in the face with exasperation.

I messaged Blake, demanding to know what was so important and yet so secretive that he couldn't tell me in front of my own father. Cowan replied within seconds, most likely because he was still up watching TV, apologising for all the angry messages. I said it was okay, feeling a massive weight being lifted off my chest. I was only just realising how much it bothered me when Cowan was mad at me. Blake, on the other hand, didn't reply.

It was as I placed my phone face down on the bedstand that the hairs along my arms stood to attention. I looked up, my gaze slowly travelling along the adjacent and opposite walls. She must be here. The corner was empty, so was the doorway, but my gaze kept being reluctantly dragged back to the window. I don't know how I knew, but it was like in a dream, when no one tells you anything, you just know.

I pushed one leg out from underneath my duvet, goose bumps erupting along my skin as I tentatively placed a bare foot on the floor, half-expecting someone to grab my leg. I attempted to push the childish nightmares down, but they crept back up and settled in the corners of my room. It was quiet, dust motes hung, their usual scattered dance suspended and everything seemed frozen in a perpetual state of delusion. I couldn't hear anything, not my heart pumping, not the blood rushing in my ears, not my ragged breath as I tried to take control of my fear. I wasn't entirely sure, as I slowly approached the window, if this was real or not, if the bang to the head had actually severed my link between reality and illusion. I reached the window, placing my hands softly on the sill.

I hoped it had.

Oh god.

I hoped this wasn't real.

Cass was standing not far beneath the window, at the front of a group. There was only four of them in total, standing close together, pale, ghostly. They were teenagers, including Cass, and they all shared that jagged, crimson slash across their throats that made my stomach drop. I gulped, fingernails digging into the wood of the sill. I didn't recognise any of them except for Cass. They all stared with the same empty gaze that made my skin crawl. It's not like they were even asking for anything. They stood there, trapped in this frozen in between world, an embodiment of my guilt. My own throat stung and I choked back a sob, my chest spasming. Pressing my fingers against the bruising, I felt the first few hot drips of blood. My breath hitched at the dark beads that balanced precariously on my fingertips. The few beads that were quickly overwhelmed by drops, then a trickle, then a stream. I stumbled backwards as it began to gush out of the gash in my throat and down the front of my pyjamas, cascading over my hands and slapping against the floor. I glanced once more at the four of them. Their faces had altered, their expressions had developed into hurt, guilt, longing. I gasped for breath as Cass began to scream. This silent, frozen world was beginning to unravel, nightmares from childhood were twisting and writhing as they fought into the edges of my vision, to block everything out. I reached out, hoping to grasp Cass one last time. Then I couldn't see, couldn't breathe anymore and collapsed back onto my bed.

I was so close to silence.

So close but for the creak of a floorboard, the swish of the air, the rustle of clothing. I squeezed my eyes shut, clenching my teeth, determined not to cry, determined not to forget their faces. Someone was in the room. But that was okay. It meant I wouldn't have to face that soul-destroying silence.

I waited, still unaware of whether I was awake or asleep, or eternally lost in that confusing state in between. The presence left, leaving an outline in my consciousness. A bird tweeted. The rising sun glinted pink. I opened my eyes.

The dust motes were dancing again in the morning light.

Chapter 12

We were at the breakfast table again, having sunk into our usual positions. Dad had his newspaper open again, but he was flicking through absently and I could tell his mind was on other things. I was resting my head in a cupped hand, the kitchen drifting in and out of focus as I struggled to stay awake. I couldn't really remember my nightmare, the only thing I could see were their faces. Every time I began to nod off, the four pairs of vacant eyes stared, non-blinking, asking for something I couldn't give them. Seeing their faces again would jolt me back into the waking world, and I'd spill my coffee. The third time I did this, Dad raised an eyebrow and I stared morosely at my mug.

I don't even like coffee.

"Maybe you should go back to bed kiddo and not worry about school," Dad had bags under his eyes too. It seemed neither of us had had a decent night's sleep, "You don't look much better. The doctor said rest remember?"

I mumbled a "Yeah, I know," but I'm not entirely sure if he heard me or not. He carried on regardless, "I'm heading into work and I'll pick up a pizza for dinner. I'll see you at five, okay?" I mumbled again, downing the last of the coffee in one vile, bitter swig. Dad sighed, and within five minutes he was slamming the front door behind him. I still hadn't moved from my seat at the breakfast table. I didn't want to go back to bed, I hated just lying there with only my thoughts for company.

I hauled myself out of the seat as Mum floated into the kitchen, "Are you sure you're well enough to go to school?" she asked, descending into Dad's seat which must have still been warm. I nodded, repressing another yawn and dropping a handful of books into my bag. I didn't even take notice if they were the ones I needed or not.

"Honey, you need to start taking better care of yourself, not getting into so many... dangerous situations,"

"Dangerous situations?" I laughed nervously, "What are you talking about?"

"A mother knows," was all she said. She seemed to wilt in her chair and I felt something slide in my chest. My old friend guilt was back. She was tapping the breakfast table with chewed fingernails, and I remembered how ill she truly was. The least I could do was put her mind at as much rest as I possibly could. "Okay mum, I promise I'll be more careful,"

I started turning away, preparing to get ready and leave for school when she half-whispered, "One last thing sweetie,"

"Yes mum?"

"Stay away from the church, and the graveyard especially. There're some dangerous people around there,"

Don't I know it.

"Of course I will," I knew I was lying when I said it, even though I desperately didn't want to be. Going back there was the last thing I wanted to do, but I knew it was going to happen. It had an inevitable call to it, like the last slice of pizza when you're full. Except a lot less fun.

"I'm gonna head up and get ready for school," I said, avoiding eye contact. Not that she would notice, she was too busy biting her nails down to the quick again, "I'll see you when I get home, okay?"

"You should listen to your father more," she called after me, "He may seem unreasonable, but he's good really,"

I was trying extremely hard not to succumb to sleep during English a few hours later. Similar to breakfast, every time I closed my eyes, the four ghosts burned on the inside of my eyelids, their slit throats glowing. I'd flinch, my elbow would slip off the table and then I'd smack my chin on the surface. The third time this happened, even the teacher (a self-obsessed, oblivious forty year old in a mid-life crisis) noticed.

Cowan was shaking with laughter when she asked if I was okay in a brief respite between her complaining about her husband and looking at her miniscule reflection in her pocket mirror.

"Just a late night," I responded. It was mostly true. The warm relief I had felt after messaging Cowan had been snuffed out by the vision of my own slit throat and the blood pouring down my front. I found my pyjamas to be clean the following morning, except for a small stain of melted chocolate from a few months ago that never came out in the wash. It still haunted me however. I stared at the borrowed textbook in front of me, filled with other people's scribbles and artistic drawings of penises: 'Macbeth'. I was beginning to understand how his wife felt.

"Found anything yet?" I asked Cowan, stifling another yawn. He was tapping away on his phone beneath the desk, absent-mindedly drumming his pen on the blank page before him, having not even glanced at the work we were supposed to be doing. And he wondered why he had to resit.

"Well you didn't give me much to work with," he complained, not even glancing up, "No names, no years. What did you think I could find?"

"I don't know, something," I buried my face in my arms, "Don't you think a number of murdered teenagers in the past ten years would be noticed by someone?" He had been searching on the local newspaper website for old articles that had any connection to murdered teens. He was currently trawling through articles of a newspaper that had been shut down a few years ago.

I ran my fingers through the tangles in my hair, "I just thought that if I could understand them better…"

"They'd go away?" Cowan finished the sentence for me. I had described my nightmare to him on the way to school and he'd been kind enough to buy me three energy drinks due to my reawakened hatred of coffee. Their effect had lasted for about half an hour before wearing off and leaving me in a more exhausted state than before. Despite the drink failing, I still felt somewhat better because Cowan had believed me without the slightest doubt.

"Yeah," I mumbled. I surveyed the classroom again, catching Courtney staring at Cowan for the fourth time that lesson. She had flung her blonde, straightened hair over her shoulder and it resembled straw more than hair. She was chatting away and sitting sideways in her seat, also oblivious to the work in front of her. And she was regularly glancing this way.

Back off.

"Y'know Courtney keeps looking at you," I observed casually.

"Uh-huh,"

"You don't think that's weird?" I sat up, surprised that it didn't seem to bother him at all. He was usually so shy, especially when it came to girls like Courtney.

"No, I told her I would explain what was going on, properly, in person,"

I felt the familiar bite of anger in my stomach. The exchange with Courtney was still fresh in my mind from last night and I didn't trust her as far as I could throw her, which wouldn't be far at all since the amount of make-up she plastered on her face would probably weigh her down.

"Has she explained?" I demanded.

"Explained what?" he was still staring at his phone, his hair hanging in front of his eyes so I could barely see his face. He wouldn't even look at me.

"About you, about why she's talking to you and who they devil worshippers are and everything…" I trailed off, hurt that he wouldn't look at me or acknowledge my concern. I knew what he was thinking, that I was jealous of Courtney. And I was, but at that time in my self-righteous and stubborn delusion, I wouldn't admit it.

"I found something," his exclamation cut through my fog of anger and my curiosity blew most of it to the back of my mind, "It's from the newspaper that was shut down seven years ago," he continued, "By Mayor Berkeley himself when he came into office. This article may possibly be the reason why,"

I leaned over his shoulder to read the headline: THIRD MURDERED TEEN. Cowan carefully placed the phone on the desk between us and we leaned closer in together to read. I felt his hair brush against my forehead and when I looked at him, the phone screen tinged his skin a pale blue. Like in the sunset the other night, he seemed to glow.

Tell him.

I focused on the article:

6th October 2009

To the dismay of the local police, a third teenager has been found brutally murdered in Raven's Wood. Dylan Finn, 16, was found half a kilometre into the woods in the same places and states as the two other recent murders of Leo Barlowe (19) and Aimee Macready (14).

A statement from Chief Inspector Stone claims they have no suspects as of yet in this investigation, but suspicion still lies at the door of the recently elected mayor Howard Berkeley.

The Finn family have been informed. "He didn't have many friends, but he was a wonderful young man who was thoughtful and perceptive," his mother claimed. His funeral will be held at the end of next week now that the investigation will be closed at the end of this week due to lack of evidence, motive and suspects.

Written by: Kathrine Moore

"What are you guys reading?" Courtney had suddenly appeared. She half sat on our desk so that her skirt hitched up and you could see where her fake tan stopped. I scowled as Cowan stuttered, glancing at her legs before making eye contact, "Oh nothing," he mumbled before almost immediately breaking it again and staring shyly at the desk. He began to write to distract himself.

"It doesn't look like nothing," she remarked, leaning over to read the phone. I stopped her before I got a full view of her cleavage.

"It's an article on why Lady Macbeth can never scrub her hands clean," I lied, promptly locking Cowan's phone and handing it back to him, "All the basic stuff really, whether it's caused by her guilt, whether it is real or just, y'know, a fantasy,"

I waited for my words to have impact, but Courtney simply assumed her famous, patronising smile and I was disappointed not to see a flash of anger behind her eyes.

"You'd tell me if you found something, wouldn't you Cowan?" she rested a chin on her hand and gazed at him, "We have to work together on this, to keep each other safe,"

I looked at Cowan, who was still fascinated by the fact ink was coming out of the end of his pen, "I think that's true enough," he conceded, turning slightly towards me, "I mean, I need to keep you safe,"

I opened my mouth, "Cowan-"

"I think you need to think about Mel too," Courtney interrupted, and I grabbed a fistful of my skirt in embarrassment at my mistake.

Cowan's head snapped up in surprise. Courtney squatted with enough grace to attract the attention of the row of boys in front. "I have something else to tell you," she whispered conspiratorially directly to me, "My brother is off limits,"

I think my eyes must have bulged out of their sockets. I blushed furiously as Courtney sauntered back to her seat. Cowan had stiffened beside me and for the first time that lesson, actually looked at me. "That isn't- it's not- it wasn't," I stumbled for the right words, too angry to explain myself properly.

"I left Courtney's early, I was mad okay?" I finally admitted, furiously, "You were texting her and I didn't feel comfortable at all, so I left and Blake followed me! I didn't do anything," Cowan didn't say anything, he simply transferred his phone back from the table between us to his lap. In fact, he didn't say anything for the rest of the lesson.

Thankfully, it came to a merciful end not long after that. I stared at the desk for the remainder, giving even less attention to Lady Macbeth and her paranoia as I tried to combat my own. Did Courtney think there was something between me and Blake? Did Cowan? For some reason, Cowan believing Courtney's implication worried me more than the idea that there were Satanists killing teenagers willy-nilly. When we were finally released from the classroom, I didn't dare look up; shame caused my face to burn like fire.

I took a quick right and was halfway down the corridor before realising that I was following a path that would directly lead me to collide with Blake Berkeley. I managed to stop myself just in time, practically skidding to a halt. The rubber squeak of my trainers on the laminated floor of the corridor immediately attracted his attention.

And the attention of Headmaster O'Donnell too.

Crap.

I felt like an intruder, invading an important meeting. They stood in a dim light since the lamp above them had broken, O'Donnell leaning over Blake ominously, despite Blake's height. A hand rested lightly bit intimidatingly on his shoulder. Blake looked mildly confused, a slight crease in between his eyebrows, but then again, that was his default setting.

And now… now they were both staring at me.

"Speak of the Devil," O'Donnell's nasally voice destroyed the sudden silence that had descended, a silence that was so out of place in a school overflowing with students. I didn't respond but I did have the sense to wipe the look of horror from my face.

"How is your father, Miss Parker?" he asked, sweeping towards me.

"Fine," I squeaked. He was leaning over me, similar to how he had been leaning over Blake, like a praying mantis about to strike. Unlike Blake however, I was much smaller. He towered over me, and I felt my knees and bladder weaken as he rested his hand gently on my shoulder. I was regretting all those energy drinks. I carefully tried to step back, in an attempt to remove his hand, but his grip only tightened and I had to bite my bottom lip to prevent a whimper.

"It's good to see him recovered after his loss," he breathed, "He seems so much better now,"

I noticed Blake's face darken as I struggled to comprehend   what O'Donnell was saying. What had Dad lost?

"I don't understand," I whispered, glancing uncomfortably at his hand. My breath caught in my throat as I realised, with a sickening jolt, that I recognised it. The same tendons creating angular ridges; the same dry and chipped nails with individual particles of dirt that I could practically count. The floor seemed to tilt beneath me and I was overwhelmed with a wave of nausea. My throat began to throb.

"It takes such effort to overcome the loss of a-"

"Mel!"

I whirled around so quick that O'Donnell finally had to relinquish his grip for fear of having his wrist snapped. Cowan stood silhouetted at the end of the corridor and I felt the same rush of gratitude as I had the first time he saved me from O'Donnell.

"We're late!" he called, signalling at me to move. O'Donnell had a look of fury on his face which intensified when Blake interjected brightly, "Yeah, we sure can't be late for Stockton!" He took me by the elbow, practically dragging me away towards Cowan.

I glanced confusedly over my shoulder and hissed at Blake, "What was he talking about?"

"It doesn't matter," he responded, staring straight ahead as if the light at the end of the corridor was a better place and not just a stupid metaphor. The three of us quickly hurried away and I felt more disorientated than ever. My throat still throbbed and now my eyes were burning and my limbs felt heavy. I figured this was my concussion haunting me worse than Cass ever could.

We left O'Donnell in the corridor, standing in semi-darkness beneath the broken light, as if he was the devil himself.

Chapter 13

Tap tap tap.

"Oh my god, can you stop that?"

A pause. Tap tap tap.

"For god's sake Cowan,"

Cowan paused again in his recital of tapping the steering wheel and said, "I'm worried,"

I looked at him, trying to decipher which current problem could be worrying him most: Cass's murderers, her hauntings, the Satanists, the fact that we were heading back to the Church, Blake.

He glanced to the side, concentrating on me for a second rather than the road and then tapped an irritating and insistent staccato.

"What exactly are you worried about? Maybe I can help,"

"I don't think there's a lot you can do," he said apologetically, "Everything is worrying me,"

"That's a lot to be worried about," I said softly, "You can't worry about everything all by yourself. C'mon, tell me a few, and I'll worry about them for you,"

He laughed at that, and it made me feel warm inside. I'd managed to make him feel better, even if it was only marginally.

"Okay," he took a deep breath, and hit the indicator to turn left into the church's carpark, "I'm worried that my school grades aren't going to be enough to get me into uni, I'm worried that I'll never be able to afford a house, I'm worried I'm going to total my car," he spoke fast, naming a worry on each click of the indicator, "I'm worried that I'm not gonna survive long enough to do any of those things and that Cass is never gonna find peace,"

He turned the steering wheel stiffly and we practically flew into the carpark. He flicked it into neutral, roughly pulling the handbrake on and sat, head down, hands shaking in his lap, "What kind of world produces people like this?"

"We're gonna get this sorted Cowan," I said decisively, "I promise you, you're gonna get into uni, your gonna buy a house and we're gonna expose these guys and allow Cass and those other kids to find peace, right? Say it,"

"We're gonna get Cass her peace," he copied hoarsely.

"Damn right we are,"

We sat in silence, the car headlights highlighting the bit of wall where we had sat on the day of Cass's funeral. We were meeting Blake who had mysteriously told us to meet him here at 5 o'clock. The dashboard now read 17:07. Why we couldn't meet during the hours of daylight was beyond me, but I hadn't seen Blake for the rest of the day, so I was pretty sure he'd skived. The only reason I had agreed to come, even with Cowan, was because Blake was finally willing to reveal the secret he had been about to tell me before Dad had arrived.

I glanced at Cowan again, and his hands hadn't stopped shaking. He seemed to be fighting with himself, an internal struggle where both sides were losing and destroying themselves.

"Cowan-"

"It was my fault," his was so quiet that it didn't register at first. My mouth was hanging open and I closed it with a snap, bewildered by the statement.

"How?"

"We had been planning your birthday and… and I let her go off on her own. I should have driven her home Mel, I always do but I let her talk me into letting her walk home and then… then she was never seen again,"

"That's not true Cowan, it was nobody's fault!" Well, it was a bit. I shifted in my seat to face him, but he wouldn't look at me. His hair fell in slashes of blonde feathers across his forehead and I could see the tears beginning to form on his eyelashes even in the dark.

Being unsure of what else to do, I interlaced my fingers with his and squeezed, "It's nobody's fault," I repeated, "I promise," Another pair of car headlights suddenly lit up the carpark in the bright, luminous light of newer headlights. Our hands were illuminated for a second in a halo of whites and blues before they were drenched in darkness again. Immediately, I let go and tumbled from the car, glad for the first time that it was dark so that no one could see the red of my cheeks.

Cowan followed suit and we surveyed the sleek BMW whose engine was idling and whose lights revealed the graveyard in a stark, clinical light, as powerful as floodlights. They made the shadows of the forest even more forbidding and dark than they already were. The few trees at the front were dull and monotone whilst the others vanished into complete and utter darkness, as if there was a black hole hidden between the trunks, sucking in and stealing the light. Anything could be lurking in there, watching us, and we simply wouldn't know.

Cowan groaned, "Great, she's here then," Blake sheepishly climbed from the passenger's side.

"I'm so sorry," he said quietly, kicking his feet and avoiding eye contact, "She'd blocked me in with her car," he nodded at the monster that was still grumbling in front of us, "I couldn't get here without asking her to move and the moment she caught the whiff of this, I couldn't get rid of her,"

"Quickly, let's go before she gets out the car," Cowan whispered just as the driver's door swung open, "Oh no, we're too late,"

Blake pulled a pack of cigarettes from his back pocket. He offered us each one, and after lots of shakings of heads, we watched him cup his hand and light it, the flame colouring his palm orange for a couple of seconds. We didn't want to look at Courtney just yet.

"You ready?" Blake puffed and the smoke curled into the night air in grey tendrils.

"I don't actually know what I'm supposed to be ready for so I guess so?" I smiled half-heartedly and Blake just nodded, his face serious and stone-like. This obviously wasn't the time nor the place for joking.

"Hey Cowan!" I felt Cowan stiffen beside me as Courtney bounded over and a small part of me rejoiced. Okay, a big part rejoiced.

"Courtney,"

"It's nice to meet up y'know, despite the circumstances," she glanced apologetically at me and I wasn't sure if she was genuinely sorry that we were meeting under such circumstances or she was just sorry that I existed. She waited, batting her eyelashes at Cowan expectantly, waiting for him to say something back. He looked pleadingly at me.

"C'mon then Blake, it's getting cold, show us what you got," I said. I wasn't lying, it was the middle of October and the cold was biting into my skin despite my hoodie.

Blake nodded again, his face of stone not slipping once. He headed for the gates and I swallowed, prepping myself to enter it again. The last time I had been on this path, it had been running full speed away from murderers who believed Satan exists. One of them had been wielding an axe. I took a deep breath and started walking. I could do this.

We passed through the gates when Blake stopped. "What is it?" I demanded. Blake turned on his heel and whispered something to Cowan who had started to follow a few feet behind us. I watched Cowan's shadowed face change from surprise to annoyance to pleading and finally to resignation.

"Blake, what is it?" I repeated. Cowan had returned to the cars and was resting against the bonnet of his car, a sulking figure of darkness between the headlights. A thoroughly put out Courtney was now looking far too smug and excited for my liking.

"Blake, why'd you do that? Why can't Cowan come?" I hissed.

Blake continued to walk away, to the newer section of gravestones, puffing absentmindedly on his fag, "I figured you may need to be alone for this,"

I sighed, "Do you want to sound anymore mysterious? You doing this on purpose or what?" He didn't respond, he was too busy counting graves, "Who are we looking for anyway?" I asked.

"You'll see,"

I felt my temper begin to fray. Important information or not, Blake couldn't treat me like this. With his deliberate vagueness and taste for drama, he was almost as bad as his sister. I dug my hands deeper into my hoodie pockets, nervously glancing at the forest every now and again, my stomach dropping in sickening fear every time a twig snapped or some leaves rustled. I understood now why they had left their headlights on, it was far easier to read the names on the gravestones using them instead of individually with a torch.

I whispered them under my breath as we passed by, "Carol Stone, loving mother and wife. Paul Robertson, a vital member of the community. Terry Marcs, 'I told you I was sick'. Sheila Matterson, taken away too early. Penny

Walker, David Graham, Joseph Vicars, Joe Smith, Ella Richards, Molly Jones, Emma-"

I stopped. I felt like someone had just whipped the ground from beneath me, like that cheap magicians trick with the table cloth, except they had got it miserably wrong and everything had gone flying and crashing and shattering and the world had tilted upside down and I was going to be sick.

Blake had also stopped and everything was so quiet compared to the deafening , ear-splitting turmoil that was going on inside my head. I could hear Blake's cigarette fizzling and crackling away to nothing, but I couldn't hear my own breathing.

"This is it," he said, his voice crawling through layers and layers of white noise in my head.

"This isn't- it can't be the same, can it?" I asked, faultering. The gravestone owner's name was written in black cursive letters that stood out against the grey marble of the stone so that there was no way you could possibly misread it:

'Emma Parker, 16th May 1972-14th October 2005, a devastating loss to her husband and child. Although gone in body, she will always remain in spirit.'

Too right she will always remain in spirit.

I choked back a sob, "Blake, what is this?"

Blake nervously lit another cigarette with trembling fingers, "Look, I hate to be the one to tell you this, but everyone kinda knows that she's dead, except you,"

"What?" I could barely get the words out. What Blake was telling me was so wrong, so alien, that they were tangling up in my throat, "That's impossible, she's at home and alive like right now,"

He shook his head sadly and kicked at the dirt, "Cass told me, 'cos she could see her too? She didn't have the heart to tell you that you mum was… well that she was dead,"

This whole entire time. Every minute, every second I had spent talking to her wasn't real, she had never been there. I couldn't believe Cass hadn't told me, that Cowan hadn't realised either.

"So everyone knows?" I whispered, "Everyone knows that my mother is dead, that she died eleven years ago when she was in hospital and I never knew? I never realised?" O'Donnell's words made sense now, "How could I be so stupid?"

I whirled around, tripping over my own feet, stumbling in my sudden desire to get away. I had to speak to Cowan, why hadn't he come with us? I needed to know if he had ever seen my mum, if he had known about this. Blake was calling after me, but I was already pounding back up the path to the carpark.

"Cowan!" I shouted, tripping clumsily every now and then, "Cowan!" I could barely see the carpark since the headlights of both cars were still lit to full brightness. But I could just make out the two shadows of Cowan and Courtney and-

And then my world fell apart all over again.

I skidded to a halt as Cowan pulled away but Courtney's hand still rested on his chest. I was on the edge of the light, still illuminated, but I could see them clearly now, their closeness, their intimacy. My stomach twisted itself into knots, plummeted and erupted into vicious butterflies within the space of seconds. I was getting sick of everyone I thought was real turning out to be fake.

Cowan swore, "Mel, please, this isn't what it-"

"Cowan!" Courtney cut across him, "This is exactly what it looks like," she argued stubbornly. Quite frankly, I didn't care.

"I need to go home Cowan," I could walk, but my fear of what was lurking in the dark overshadowed my anger for now.

"What did Blake-"

"Take me home," I sounded rude and ungrateful but Cowan wasn't allowed to finish a sentence.

"You can't speak to him like that!" Courtney's voice was no longer harmonious, but was now a distant whining beneath the buzzing inside my skull. My mind was beginning to shut down, it couldn't cope with any new information, with any new shocks.

I pulled the door open savagely. I slipped into seat, sitting on my hands to stop them from shaking. Blake had reappeared at the gates and was leaning against, possibly smoking his third. He had a faint smile playing on his lips as he watched Courtney and Cowan.

I could hear Courtney's voice and my nails dug into my thighs in anger. It grated against my ear drums and I opened my mouth to shout at Cowan to hurry up when he started to yell. It was so loud. I glanced at the treeline, frightened that his shouting would attract someone, but it remained empty. Blake was grinning widely now, happily smoking away as he watched the entertainment. Cowan's bellow was so loud that I could barely make out what he was saying. There were a couple of choice swearwords and insults, but I was too frazzled to really listen to what he was saying.

Minutes later we were speeding away down the road. Cowan had left a crying Courtney in his dust. We didn't say anything, we were both scared of the other. I was still fuming over what he did, but I was too scared to actually say anything in case he started yelling again.

We pulled up outside my house in record time and we just sat there, unsure of what to do. I looked up at my house and to my horror saw Mum walk past the window, dressed in a simple white shift. How had I not known?

"What did Blake tell you?" Cowan's voice broke the fragile silence between us. I felt the fires of my temper beginning to flicker into life again.

"My mother died eleven years ago," I said, watching her pass back and forth in front of the window aimlessly, "Did you know?"

"You mean you didn't?"

My anger fried every other emotion inside me, "What the hell Cowan? I talk about her all the time, how did you not pick up on this?" I demanded.

"Oh what, I'm expected to know what's going on inside that thick head of yours?"

God, if only you did.

"I expect you to have at least a little consideration for my feelings,"

We glared at each other, our breath coming in sharp gasps of fury.

I was beginning to struggle with the door's lock and my seatbelt, attempting to undo both at the same time in my haste when Cowan said softly, "There was this one time where you made two cups of tea even though I'd said I didn't want one. You then placed it on the dining table and we went into the lounge and you acted like it was completely normal so y'know, I never questioned it. I put it down to exam stress,"

I froze, and I couldn't stop the tears from spilling. I'm officially crazy.

He reached up, wiped a stray tear from my cheek. I looked in his eyes, his pupil as black as the forest had been, ringed in icy blue. And I saw him and Courtney reflected there, their intimate embrace seared into my mind, an image that I would never be able to get away from.

I got out the car and I told him in no uncertain terms to "eff" off.

Chapter 14

I couldn't find Mum or Dad, not that I had looked very hard. I didn't want to see either of them. I was scared of what I would find if I did look. I felt like my insides had been hastily scooped out with a dirty spade and left behind in an untidy pile somewhere at the church. Maybe I would go back and find them, find the feelings that I was supposed to be experiencing right now. But I couldn't move for my numbness.

Courtney had kissed Cowan.

Cowan had kissed Courtney.

Right in front of me and this was the only thing I was really overly concerned with. Not that my mother was dead, not that my best friend was dead, not that we had her murderers after us, but the fact that some dumb, blonde, stereotypical high schooler with a big rack had kissed Cowan. What the hell was wrong with me?

What was I supposed to do? I cocooned myself, resentfully admitting that Dad was right. I should have stopped talking to Cowan when he told me to. Maybe I should have had more friends because at least then I would have had someone to turn to.

I must have drifted off into sleep or something because reality came into crushing focus all of a sudden, cars on the road, birds outside, the sound of my own breathing, all punctuated by a persisting tapping on the glass of my mirror. It reminded me of Cowan tapping his steering wheel to annoy me. I knew who it would be before I even pulled the covers back.

Cass was standing, staring at me. This was... what? The ninth time she had appeared to me in her spectral form? Why couldn't she just leave me alone? She was exactly the same as I had seen her every other time. Her clothes hadn't changed, her buttons still reflected the light like miniature suns, her curly ginger hair was still a wild mess. The cut on her throat was as lividly bright as ever. I was sick of the tumult of emotions that I felt every time I saw her. Grief, guilt, and unbearable sadness. But this was all crushed by an insufferable rage at what had happened to her, and what Cowan had done, and how bloody well done I was with it all.

"Go away Cass," I said, retreating back under the covers, "Just die already,"

Yet, there was something different. She hadn't looked precisely, unerringly, exactly the same.

She had been smiling.

I peeked suspiciously out again, and she was still there, smiling and tapping relentlessly in the glass. My mouth dropped open, what had changed? I scrabbled and fought with the duvet to get it off me and tumbled out of bed. I practically crawled across the floor because I couldn't get to the mirror fast enough. I stared at her, and suddenly her face was animated, filled with feelings that I seemed to have lost.

She opened her mouth and I thought she was screaming again so my breath caught in my throat. But she indicating with her finger, making motions on the glass and I suddenly realised what she was getting at. We used to play this game, despite our age, where we would breathe on the glass and draw doodles in our breath. It eventually moved on to ruder images, but we still used to play it every now and again. So that's what I did, I breathed all over the glass and she began to write in it.

'Cowan doesn't like Courtney.' was the first thing she wrote. I scowled, the topic of Cowan and Courtney being the last thing I wanted to talk about.

"Don't we have more pressing matters to talk about?" I wiped away her words and breathed again.

'This is important.'

"How can you be so sure of that? It takes two to kiss! In fact," I checked my phone, scrolling through the dozens of messages from Cowan, most of them furious, "He has just buggered off back to the church with her. How romantic,"

'You don't think that's odd?'

"What? That they're going to the church together?"

Cass nodded vigorously, then wrote in the glass again. Her writing became more of a scrawl as she agitatedly swept her fingertips over the glass, 'Wanna know why I went there? Blake and I got close (she looked embarrassed at this point, shy even) I got a message from him, but really-' She had to stop writing because she had run out of room. I rapidly wiped it down and breathed all over it. She carried on writing: 'it was from Courtney. I did, suspecting nothing and she was there. It's her, she's the one getting the victims there, her Dad is running it.'

My head suddenly started to pound, blood pumping through my head, resounding through my ear drums like a relentless heartbeat. There was so much noise, I couldn't breathe, I couldn't see, I couldn't make a single noise. It was like hanging from the tree again. The sheer amount of panic threatened to crush me.

Then it stopped.

Everything was silent, except for a lone bird calling as it settled in for the night. I swayed on the spot, stared at the mirror glass. Cass was gone. But she had left a message.

COWAN'S NEXT.

Before I knew it, I was on the phone to Cowan. New feelings that I now realise were actually old ones were bubbling ferociously in my chest, making me do things without thinking. It rang twice before being cut off on the third ring. I couldn't believe it, he'd purposely ignored my call. I rang three more times and the same thing happened. I looked at Cass's words and my heart started pumping at what seemed like a mile a minute. But really it was Courtney. I bashed out a hurried message to his phone: 'I swear Courtney, if this is you, you'll regret it.' It was a pretty pathetic threat, one that didn't hold that much menace but I didn't have to time to think of one that would strike the fear of God into her.

I called Blake next and he picked up on the second ring, "'Sup,"

"Is Courtney with you?"

"Is she ever with me?"

"Seriously,"

"I'll check her room," I nervously drummed my fingers on my dresser, all my thoughts on that stupid boy, as I heard Blake move about and open a door. I groaned when I heard him swear.

"She's not here, she must have left after she dropped me off,"

So Cowan mustn't have been lying when he said they'd gone to the church. I realised now that I never truly believed that Cowan was capable of lying to me, the same way I could never lie to him.

"I think she's gone back to the church," I quickly explained, "With Cowan. I think he's in danger,"

"Are you not crazy mad at him right now though?"

"Unbelievably furious," I replied cheerfully, "But that doesn't mean I want him to die so I could really do with a lift to the church right now,"

"I'll be ten minutes," He hung up and I quickly pulled a hoodie over my pyjamas and slipped into a pair of trainers that I found easy to run in. I checked the time – 19:21 – and tucked my phone into my pocket and danced wildly in a circle for a minute, looking for some sort of viable weapon. There was nothing in here that could cause any damage so I hurtled down the stairs and into the lounge, heading straight for the fireplace.

There was a metal poker next to it and I pulled it out of its stand, hefting it in my hand to test its weight. It felt good, I finally had some means to protect myself. And him if need be.

"Melanie, what in God's name are you doing?"

Although I wasn't sure if it would protect me from ghosts.

Mum stood in the doorway, barely filling it with her slight frame. Ashamed of myself, I held the poker up with a trembling hand and said, "You're dead,"

I watched her face crumple, and my anger at her deception that I had lived to so ignorantly in melted away. She turned away and ran and I felt like a monster. A tantrum-throwing, malicious little monster. I dashed after her, calling, "Mum? Mum please, I'm sorry!" I searched desperately around the hallway, the landing the kitchen but she had vanished.

It was as I was standing in the middle of the hallway shouting for my mother that Dad came through the door. "What the Devil are you doing?" he asked bewildered. He had frozen by the front door, key still in the lock and I saw Blake pull up in the road behind him. So much for being home for 5 with pizza. I thought of how I had never seen Blake in the driver's seat of a car before and then wondered if he even had a provisional.

The poker hung limply in my hand and I realised how ridiculous I must have looked in my pink 'hello kitty' pyjamas, crying for my mum.

"How could I have not known Dad?" I questioned, struggling to stop myself from crumbling into pieces of madness, "How could I have not realised?"

"Mel, honey, what are you talking about?"

"Did Mum ever come back from the hospital?"

I watched in infinite detail, as if someone had switched on the slow-motion, as the blood drained from his face, as his expression turned slack and his shoulders slumped. That told me all I needed to know. She never had come out of that hospital. Not alive anyway.

I brushed past him as he was still frozen at the door, clutching it so tightly that his knuckles had turned white enough to see the veins underneath, "I have somewhere to be," I said, swinging the poker onto my shoulder, "I'll call you later,"

It would have been far more dramatic if I hadn't tripped on a loose brick in the driveway.

Chapter 15

I watched Blake as he drove. He didn't drive like Cowan who was all fluid movements. He changed gears with jerky, nervous actions. I was becoming more and more suspicious that he couldn't actually drive.

"Blake, have you got a licence?"

"What? Yeah, totally," He paused for a moment as he concentrated on changing gear and then admitted, "I've had six lessons," I was too concerned with what might be happening to Cowan than the immediate danger I was in. My leg jiggled nervously as I eyed the speedometer that rarely strayed above 30mph. I felt conflicted: I felt relief that Blake wanted to be safe but we were on a national speed limit road. I needed to get to Cowan.

We finally crawled into the church carpark and only Courtney's car was there. It was parked in the darkest corner and seemed like even more of a menacing beast than usual. I was out of the car before Blake had even put it into neutral or pulled the handbrake on.

I was halfway down the path when Blake finally caught up with me. I was using my phone's torch which only provided a pitiful little circle of light when Blake flicked on what appeared to be an almost industrial standard torch. The entire forest ahead lit up, from roots to the tips of the top of the trees. The forest was a lifeless, monotonic image. The torch drained everything of its colour and we walked into the forest, dead pine needles and sticks crackling under our feet. The feeling of us stumbling into a netherworld returned and I had to swallow my fear. I was here for Cowan. Even if he was a jerk.

"Do you know where they are?" Blake asked. He had passed the torch to me and was fumbling with a fag again.

"I know exactly where they are," I said grim-faced. I noticed the trees grow closer. They were densely packed

105

and even with the torch on, we could barely see a few metres in front. I flicked it off and plunged us into darkness.

"What'd you do that for?" Blake hissed as he burned his fingers with his lighter.

"We'll just announce that we're here shall we?" I hissed back. I pushed through the trees and Blake followed. In the distance I could just make out the flickering, hypnotising light of the fire. It was like the flame that Blake's lighter created, small and entrancing, attractive enough to make you want to touch it but dangerous enough to hurt you. I felt drawn to it like I was to the flames ahead and I supposed that this was exactly what the worshippers felt like. All that money and power did sound attractive… too bad it came at the cost of your soul.

We kept moving, and I vaguely recognised the area where Cowan and I had hid a few days ago. There was the rock that I had banged my head on. In the shadows, I saw a piece of fabric stretched between branches and I realised it was the scarf that I lost.

I forced my way forward, ignoring the sudden skipping of my heart and the sudden hitching of my breath. I was utterly terrified of what I might find but I couldn't stop. I couldn't be that pathetic little wimp that was scared of a whisper of wind through the hedges outside her house or that flinched whenever the toaster finished anymore. It was time to pull myself together.

The path continued to narrow and the branches and brambles and shrubs leaned in closer, grasping and grabbing at our clothing as if they were trying with all their might to stop us from moving forward. I heard Blake continually muttering and swearing under his breath, slipping continuously and I thought about how impractical it would be for people in large black cloaks to make their way through this.

Eventually, the trees started to thin a bit. The frozen world of perpetual darkness was pushed back by the fire, dancing dust motes flickering on the edge. It was crackling at the centre of a circle of decrepit sandstone tombs, nearly entirely smothered by ivy and brambles. However, someone had hacked and chopped at it to create the clearing, to create space for the fire and space for worshipping.

I started to move faster, ignoring Blake's pitiful, "Wait up," as I started smacking leaves and branches out of the way, tripping over roots and dodging around trees. I was so close, so very near. A few more metres, a few more steps and he would be there. The trees were fighting back with a vengeance now, scraping my palms and grazing my face and I tripped, bouncing of a tree trunk before I was running again without even breaking my stride and I'd be able to yell at him for being a jerk and for kissing Courtney even though it didn't matter anymore because if I could yell at him that would mean he was safe and alive and-

I stumbled into the clearing, covered in mud and blood, shaking and gasping. The fire was blazing and the sheer heat of it made it difficult for me to catch my breath. Blake tumbled in after me and his face flushed red in the sudden heat, melting into the same colour as his checked shirt. Despite the fact that it was the middle of October and late at night, I couldn't feel the cold.

I still shivered though.

Cowan was sat with his back leaning against a grave, his hands bound behind him. The sight of him made my knees buckle, my stomach lurch, my heart break. For a single second, my entire body stopped and I felt as if I was falling. Falling through the cracks that fractured my reality, falling into the darkness of despair at the thought of losing Cowan, falling into the depths of hell itself. He'd taken a beating and his head was lolling a little as he tried to focus on us. Courtney was leaning over him, fumbling with the ties behind him, tears streaming down her face. She whirled around when she heard the crack of the branches, shouted as us, and then carried on trying to untie him.

"I found him like this! We need to get away, they're still here, I know it," her breath came in shaking gasps and her chest heaved with the effort. Blake and I moved around the fire and I rushed to Cowan. I skidded on my knees when I reached him, tearing a sizeable hole in the knee of my pyjama bottoms on the solid dirt ground, adding to the dozens of nicks already scattered across them.

I held his face in my hands. His bleeding, bruised face.
I need to help him-
"Cowan," I said softly, "Why'd you do it Cowan?"
I need to-
He mumbled something a bit of blood trickled from between his lips.

I-

"Oh god, what have they done to you," my hands trembled as I wiped it away.
I can't do anything-
He's gonna die-
He tried again and managed a weakened, "Run,"
"Hell no,"
"Courtney's-"
"Oh my god Cowan! You're awake, oh my god," Courtney's shriek made me wince, it was off key and loud. She leaned in for another kiss, elbowing me out of the way in the process and that seemed to kick Cowan into

108

motion. Courtney had loosened his binds enough so that he could flick his hands out, one into her throat, the other into her chest.

"Jesus, leave me alone," he spluttered blood.

Courtney bristled, blood splattered her clothes and her face, "How dare you," she hissed. She was on her feet in seconds, shaking with rage, "Don't tell me you prefer this bitch?" she demanded.

Cowan struggled to his knees, ignoring her and I tucked an arm around my neck to support him.

I glowed with pride.

I had several insults in mind, ready to take her down a peg or two. But she persisted with her ranting, so I focused on holding Cowan up. He'd obviously taken a beating all over, he clutched his ribs and I could hear his breath rattling around in his chest.

Courtney was pointing at me, "I don't believe this! You're all so blind!" I stared at her, trying to figure out what she was shouting about now, "That weirdo! I mean look at her. Bloody listen! How have you missed it? It's so obvious!" Courtney screeched, her usual perfect composure utterly shattered like a precious Ming vase. I glanced around anxiously, worried that they would come back.

"Courtney shut up!" I growled, heaving Cowan onto the grave where he collapsed.

"Idiots! Mel's possessed!"

 She's wrong, you're not.

I closed my mouth that had opened of its own accord to argue back. But everything clicked into place. That voice in my head: that sarcastic, rude, controlling voice. The one that simply couldn't accept that Cass was gone, that continually brought her to the forefront of my mind. It wasn't me. It wasn't even me.

It had been Cass the entire time.

"Bitch!" Courtney stumbled back, taken by surprise by my ferocity and possibly by the fact that no one had ever spoken to her like that before. But I wasn't even speaking to her. All my anger was aimed at Cass. Sneaky, lying little-

I'm sorry.

"Get out!" I continued to scream, "Get out, get out, get out," I was gripping my head, pulling at my hair, scratching and scrabbling, trying to get rid of her. Never had I felt so betrayed. Courtney had stopped yelling and Blake was standing next to her now. He dropped his cigarette to the floor, snuffed it out with the heel of his boot and turned to his sister, "I think they're ready now,"

I barely heard him, barely comprehended what he had said. He had betrayed us? Betrayed Cass more than anyone. All that crap he had sprouted about taking them down was lies, he had been lying from the start and I was stupid to trust him. I was stupid to trust anyone. My mind was a tumult of thoughts and feelings, unwrapping into turmoil, coursing around my head in white water rapids but in a whirlwind as well and I just thought the same thing over and over and over- then suddenly it was silent.

She must have left.

Around the clearing, they had gathered. I slowly straightened, my back aching. There were dozens of them, all dressed in the same black cloaks, drifting in between the trees like ghosts. It was surreal and I once again wondered how they weren't ripping their cloaks on any of the branches whilst I had been nearly torn to shreds. They entered the clearing and I was reminded of Hot Fuzz except we didn't have any guns and this wasn't a comedy.

Blake and Courtney had donned their black cloaks.

Of course. Fakers.

I was falling down the cracks now. The small fractures of my reality had burst right open thanks to betrayal after betrayal and revealed a bottomless, hopeless pit. I was thoroughly prepared to give in. I wouldn't be able to save Cowan now, I wouldn't be able to help Cass. They pressed around Cowan and I, creating a tight circle of black, hooded bodies.

I was done.

Countless faces that I knew and that I didn't. O'Donnell, Huang from the hospital, a handful of councilmen, the Chief of Police, Damien Stone. Ah, Damien. The gruff voice on the other end of the phone from Friday came back to me and I felt defeat wash over me in a tsunami sized wave. Damien had called the house. "It wasn't just the Micheals kid, yours too," Damien had called Dad.

I give up.

Berkeley stepped forward, theatrically flicking the hood of his cloak off his head, charisma practically oozing out of his pores. I finally understood how he had reached Mayor. He smiled, all sweaty skin and jowly lips and yellow teeth. After everything this man and his people had done, after murdering kids, after murdering Cass, after hurting us again and again and again and luring us here to kill us too, this man was able to smile.

It was over.

If Cowan hadn't risen to his feet like an outdated zombie it probably would have been.

"You stay away from us," he growled through gritted his teeth. It was then that I noticed that he'd been hit so hard that he was missing an incisor. He was swaying, but he managed to hold his ground.

111

"I'm afraid you are not the one to be giving orders Michaels," Berkeley announced. The circle came closer, encircling and trapping us next to the gravestone. Those that stood before the fire were just black silhouettes and I remembered the dancing figures from a couple of nights ago, they were burned onto my retinas. "This silly little game that you and Miss Parker have played has come to an end. We can't have people like you tainting the earth with your heathen and disturbing powers,"

"What's he talking about?" I whispered. I knew I was supposed to feel fear, that some animal instinct should have kicked in and made me want to survive. But I felt numb and I had a sneaking suspicion that it was because Cass had gone. She had always been so much more stubborn and determined than me. I heard her voice, "You give up too easy,"

"What do you mean?" Cowan demanded.

"Don't pretend that you don't know Michaels, you know exactly what I'm talking about. It's time to purge the planet of your blasphemous footsteps," Berkeley raised his hands and took the position of a preacher, and some of worshippers began to chant.

"But we haven't done anything,"

"You've communicated with the unclean, the undead, the abominations that don't belong to this world," he declared, "It is our job to exterminate you and keep our planet clean. It is our duty to do the deeds of the Devil!" It was like the twisted version of a church ceremony on a Sunday. Berkeley took the position of the pastor, ranting about the work of the Devil to the heavens as the chanting reached a crescendo around him.

"Please, we don't understand, we haven't done anything," Cowan cried, begged, pleaded, "We're just kids! God, have a bit of mercy!" He was actually making an effort to get us out of his nightmare whilst I stood there, dazed and emotionless.

"O'Donnell, it is your turn to do the honours," Berkeley indicated to the tallest of the figures who glided forward and Berkeley continued, "Son, you did such a good job last time. You take the Parker girl," Berkeley was still grinning his manic smile and it tore his face in two in an ugly gash.

Cowan's begging switched tactics and he grabbed my arm, pulling me behind him and I felt warmth rush up my arm. His grip was weak, but his nails still dug in, "Please don't hurt her, please," He hugged me close, keeping me away from Blake as he detached from the crowd.

The numbness that had wrapped me up in an unfeeling bundle was beginning to fall away as I realised what Cowan was doing. "Oh no," I whispered, "You can't do this Cowan," I argued, "I came here to save you," The numbness evaporated, my emotions rushing in, all the pain and fear and hurt and it came crashing into me and everything was suddenly running at twice the speed, "No, please!"

Cowan and I were pulled apart. O'Donnell pulled him away by the neck of his jumper and he was too weak to really fight it. Blake had me around the chest and I found that I had the energy to fight like a bobcat, all claws and nails and teeth. The growing warmth that had begun to course through my body was ebbing already. Cowan and I were gripping each other with just our fingers and I was begging and screaming and the tears were coming and our fingers were slowly slipping like a clichéd romance novel. A sharp jab to Cowan's ribs from O'Donnell saw an end to that. We were dragged a couple of feet apart and I was still fighting and screaming but I could see Cowan flagging, his punches and slaps barely having an effect.

"Who's first?" Huang asked, as efficient as ever.

Berkeley tapped his chin, causing the flesh of his cheek to wobble. His movements were slow and deliberate, no longer the spasming, birdlike twitches that I was used to. He glared at me and I stopped fighting to glare back and once again our eye contact fizzled in the air between us. We were back at the dinner table. "Oh shut up you stupid little man!" I could see that he remembered it too.

"Parker," his smile grew wider, "Parker first,"

Cowan suddenly went wild, bucking and jumping and bellowing, "Don't you dare! Don't hurt her! I'm begging you, she's got nothing to do with this. Leave her alone! Please! I'm begging. please!" His words were mingling with his sobs and my screams.

O'Donnell towered above him, even though they were the same height, "Be silent!" he thundered, sparks flying in the night air around him so he looked like he had just clambered out of hell.

"I won't!" Cowan retorted, "I won't stop, not until you let her go!" This was so unlike Cowan. His hair was swept back and I could see his face so clearly. Despite the fact a murderer had him by the scruff of his jumper, despite the danger of imminent death, his eyes were still bright and defiant. And I realised then, amongst this craziness and darkness and violence and utter madness, that I loved him.

Nice timing.

But Blake was dragging me across the dirt, my sneakers kicking up mud and dead leaves. The chanting was only getting louder and the fire was burning brighter and Blake socked me in the jaw and I saw stars and then he picked up a rock.

Oh god.

I was crying like a toddler as he pushed me onto the grave. Tears and snot and spit all mixing into one slimy mess. Quite frankly, I didn't want to be killed with a rock and I just couldn't control myself. I was still struggling against Blake, but suddenly this lanky pothead had the strength of a thousand men. He leaned in, his breath heavy and stinking with cigarette smoke and pushed my forehead into the slab of sandstone, "Y'know I killed her right?" he laughed and I realised with sinking dread that he was just as mad as his father, if not more so, "I worked on her for six months, waiting for her to trust me just as much as you and the slut fell for it. I sacrificed her,"

And then I saw red. I don't remember what I screamed, who I kicked, who I hissed and spat at but after a few minutes of a complete loss of control, I was being pressed hard into the stone, three of four bodies holding me down. Despite the fact that my blood was still boiling, I couldn't move. I had exhausted myself, having channelled every last bit of energy into my final attempt to break free.

And I'd failed.

"Please," I gasped. I could hear Cowan yelling in the background, and he was crying too. They murmured something and for one hopelessly futile moment, I thought I had got through to them. Then Blake laughed again and he bought the rock down, smashing it against my skull.

The world went silent.

I wasn't sure if I was dead or...

Oh no, here came the pain. It rocked around my skull like a power drill, boring into my brain, my teeth, my eyes. They rattled within their sockets. There was a high pitch whining like a dentist drill and I knew I was screaming, my throat felt like it was tearing itself apart, but I couldn't hear it. I couldn't see anything, it was all dark except for a few blindingly bright lights at the corners of my vision. I didn't bother to wonder if this was what it was like to die. I wasn't ready for it, whatever it was.

Then suddenly I could feel strong arms picking me up. My head lolled, my breath was rasping. I could just hear a voice coming from miles away, "Mel, sweetie, my beautiful girl. It's gonna be okay, you listen now, you'll be fine,"

"Dad?" I managed.

And then I blacked out.

Chapter 16

The first thing I woke to was a blissful ignorance as my concussed state prevented me from remembering what had happened. But even in that wonderful state, I could sense dark, brooding clouds waiting at the peripheral of my consciousness. I tried to stay in my sunny little bubble that didn't have ghosts or dead friends or Satanists, but nothing could stop the thunderous storm of my memories from bursting through.

My eyes flew open and I gasped, certain that I was going to find myself still in the forest. I looked around vaguely for the towering pines, but all I could make out was a white Styrofoam ceiling divided into so many squares that it made my head ache.

Speaking of my head...

I sat up slowly, inviting a wave of nausea and tentatively touched the back of my head. It had been wrapped in several layers of bandages which had been tightly wound across my forehead and above my ears, pushing them down and making them stick out. It somehow made me feel safer; no one could reach my wound without having to go through several layers of medical tape and cotton.

I tapped tentatively around, establishing that I was in a bed and persistent beeping to my left told me that I was alive and back in the hospital. Lisa Huang sauntered into my mind and I finally found my animal instincts telling me to get away. I pushed myself upwards and slumped back on the pillows, waiting as the room slipped in and out of focus. Everything seemed to have a shadow, a copy of itself. I think I had double vision due to my concussion.

I head a soft murmur to my right, "She's awake,"

I looked around and saw two Cowans and I couldn't help but smile. Somehow I managed to focus and they merged back into one. He smiled shyly, "Hi,"

"You're okay?"

It might have been my drug addled brain or possibly the concussion but he seemed to hesitate before nodding slowly, "Yeah, I'm fine,"

A frail, wobbly figure was sitting next to Cowan, her hands clasped in her lap. She wore a white summer dress, lined with lace, despite the fact that it was October.

"Mum?"

"Hey sweetie," She got up and sat beside me, her edges disappearing into a fuzziness so that I struggled to see her. I reached out and my hand passed right through her. I pretended it was my concussion and my natural lack of hand-eye coordination. I pretended that she was really here. That she was really alive.

"Mum, I'm so sorry,"

She held up her hand and I noticed that her nails were bitten down to the quick. Now that I thought about it, they had always been like that, I suppose they had never grown. "None of that matters," she said with more authority in her voice than I had ever heard from her before.

"But-"

"No, you've had a nasty accident Mel,"

"I know what happened," I whispered fiercely.

Mum sighed and a look of sadness so painful crossed her face that my stomach bunched into knots.

"What's important," Cowan interjected, changing the subject, "Is that you're alright,"

"What about you?" I argued back, my voice rasping in my throat, cracking slightly with concern. It sounded like it belonged to an elderly lady who struggled to kick a 20-

a-day habit, "Are you alright? What happened, how did you get away?"

The stream of questions exhausted me and I almost missed Cowan's sheepish glance at my mother. I collapsed back into the pillows, waiting for an answer. A headache was beginning to form, pounding at my forehead, squeezing my eyes, coiling tightly around my wound.

Mum's words sounded as if I was at the bottom of a pool, and the water was trapping her words in bubbles that were floating away just out of reach. She was fading as my headache grew stronger. "There's something we need to explain…" she began at the same time that someone started to bang horrendously on the door.

Oh god, they've found me.

Cowan's sheepish glance at my mother.

"There's something we need-"

Oh no. Oh god, please no.

I looked around wildly, panicking, when I realised that the horrendous pounding on the door was actually only a gentle tapping, emphasised by my headache. Conflicting thoughts fought in my mind, the immediate problem of someone at the door and the other immediate problem of Cowan.

Mum stood and retook her place next to Cowan in the corner, out of the way of the door. I pressed the heels of my hands into my eyes, trying in a vain attempt to alleviate the pain in my head, to try and stop my thoughts leading me to terrifying conclusions.

The door swung open and I stared in bewilderment as six people entered the room two at a time, like Noah's ark. I blinked in confusion for a second at the fact that each person had a clone before establishing that it was my double vision playing tricks. I shook my head, trying to focus, but it only made things worse.

The first person I focused on was Dad, looking forlorn and dejected as he slumped into a chair next to me. I didn't dare look at him for too long, unable to get the phone call out of my head and the fact that he was connected to this madness. Instead, I concentrated on the other four figures who merged into Lisa Huang and Chief of Police Damien Stone. This was also a mistake.

I struggled to prevent myself from vomiting.

They were here to kill me, I was sure of it.

"We're here to see if you remember anything from your," she paused for a breath, hesitating so subtly that I barely saw it, "accident,"

If I remember anything? I remember everything! I wanted to scream, to tell them that I knew exactly who they are and what kind of monsters they've become. It was like a giant elephant had just lumbered into the room, pooped on the floor and then rolled around in it and everyone was still ignoring it.

"I don't remember much," I lied, desperately trying to figure out how I could find my way out of this. They were the ones who claimed it was an accident, but what kind of accident? "Only that we were going to Raven's Wood, to meet Cowan and Courtney," I glanced at Cowan, "That's right isn't it?" I asked him.

He only nodded.

Stone looked confused and Huang frowned and I realised my mistake instantly, having fallen into an old habit so easily. "Blake was-" I forged on loudly, faultering on purpose and driving their attention away from what I just said, "Blake was driving. He hasn't got his licence yet. That's all I remember? What happened, did we crash?" I asked innocently.

My headache was becoming more intense, like a deaf builder had decided to put his drill up to maximum because he couldn't tell the difference. They knew I was lying and I had to stifle a snort as they agreed, saying that the car had overturned on one of the corners and that I had a nasty bump to the head.

Dad's voice cut through, "Leave her be,"

"You know we can't," Huang turned him, acting now as if I wasn't even there, "There are signs Marcus, she's one of them," One of who? I thought about Berkeley and his preaching, how he wanted to eliminate us so that he may do the work of the Devil and purge the Earth. What made us so different? I tried to think about it, but my head was killing me. I didn't care anymore, I just wanted the pain to stop.

Dad rose, his height all of a sudden greater than I had ever seen it, taller than Cowan, taller than O'Donnell even. He was imposing and intimidating and this underlying power of his explained how he had gained influence over these people. They craved power like his. "I said leave her be Huang," he growled.

"But who was she talking to?" I had always assumed that Stone had been a blundering fool, incapable of solving any major crime since he had done such a poor job at solving Cass's. Of course, it was apparent to me now that he was very good at his job, he had simply chosen not to find Cass's killer. Which kind of made a lot of sense.

His words sparked a fuse of anger inside me however and I interrupted loudly, "I was talking to..." and promptly trailed off at the furious look on Dad's face. I was beginning to understand what so-called 'powers' we had that made them want to kill us. Talking to the dead wasn't a common ability I guess.

"Myself?" I finished lamely.

Huang reluctantly wrote this down, "No delusions or hallucinations?" she tried, trying to keep the desperation out of her voice.

I didn't dare look at Mum nor Cowan either, a terrible pip of truth settled in the pit of my stomach, causing it to churn and the wave of nausea to return. "I'm seeing double," I admitted, "And I've got a really bad headache. Does that count?"

Stone groaned and mumbled something about having more important business elsewhere and left the room. Huang looked equally strained, "We'll prescribe you some more medication for the headache and double vision, most likely caused by your concussion. Be sure to let us know if you remember anything,"

I went to nod, but the slight tilt of my head sent shooting pains exploding behind my eyes so mumbled an "okay," instead. As if I was going to take anything they would give me.

As soon as she had left, and the door had been shut firmly, I rounded on my father, "Why can't they see them?" I demanded, already knowing the answer just not wanting to admit. Not Cowan, anyone but Cowan.

Dad sighed, collapsing heavily back into the chair. The power and influence he had just exhibited moments before had vanished and he looked beaten, "Honey," he said, running a hand through his hair, "I can't see them either,"

I couldn't look at Cowan. At least with Mum I had been prepared but not Cowan. In those five simple words, my world was blown apart. Everything. Gone. Everyone I loved, Mum, Cass, Cowan, they were all dead. I tried to say something, anything, but all that came out, to my shame, was a choked sob. Yet inside, I was so angry. What the hell had I done to deserve this? Why was I the one who ended up with this pathetic yet terrifying and murderous man for a father?

Pull yourself together!

I gripped the bed sheets, clenching and unclenching my fists to control my breathing. Unfortunately, my hands were trembling so my breath came out in shaking gasps too. I was furious that she had the audacity to come back, but secretly relieved too. It was my only connection to her, some people would kill for an opportunity like this. In fact, a person like that was sitting beside me right now.

"You're dead?" I managed in a half-whisper, directed mostly at Cowan, "Since when?"

Dad looked momentarily confused at the question before he realised who I must have been talking to. His bemusement quickly morphed into earnestness and yearning and it made me sick, "Is she here?" he asked desperately.

"Who?"

"Your mother,"

"Dad, I don't understand! She's always been here, since breakfast the other day, since Cass died, since she came back from..." I don't know why I was arguing anymore. I remembered the argument that Cowan and I had had last night, or the night before or whenever it was. That stupid, pointless argument about Cowan not knowing about my feelings when I didn't even know myself. I'd wasted my precious last few minutes with him. And as for mum...

Dad had told me she was ill. Not like 'she'll better after some rest and cough syrup' ill but like mentally 'she may never get better' ill. For me to learn now, in finality, that she never recovered, that the mother I actually have is a simply a ghost and that my two only friends had now joined her, well, how was I supposed to act?

I don't think anyone, least of all me, expected my sudden calmness.

"She never came home did she," I stated, in final confirmation of all the evidence I had, the gravestone, the fact that she could simply disappear, that I had never actually hugged her in ten years. How could I have not noticed any of this?

I looked at Dad and I saw myself escape this delusion in his eyes. He turned away, staring at the hospital tiles but he wasn't seeing them. His eyes were rimmed red, puffy and empty, his skin pale and blotchy under the harsh illumination of the lights. He was silent for what seemed an age before he began to explain.

"Do you remember the first time your mother checked into the psychiatric hospital? About twelve years ago. You came to wave her off and I remember it was the same day that you first met Cass. Technically, your mother never checked out again. She died due to gross negligence, no one was paying attention, she got worse and she forgot about you and me and-" he stopped when he saw my bottom lip trembling.

"Anyway," he continued, "I was too devastated, too scared to tell you at first. When I did, you just nodded and carried on with whatever you were doing. You took it remarkably well,"

"But all this," he waved a hand despondently, indicating the entire predicament where we now found ourselves, "All of this is my fault. I couldn't bare to be without your mother. The biggest mistake I made was to confide in Huang, who had been one of the only good carers for your mother at the time,"

Mum started to cry silently in the corner and I couldn't bare to look at her as she sobbed into her hands. My chest was slowly being ripped apart, my heart being torn away in strips.

"She was the one who dragged me into it, and although I'm not shifting blame, if it wasn't for her we probably wouldn't be here. She dragged me into some sort of worship to the Devil and it was just the two of us at first. I was grieving so terribly that I didn't even notice. And then things got a little bit crazy,"

He paused and glanced at me, "You following?"

I nodded coldly, "You were grieving, joined a devil cult and things still managed to get crazy?"

"We summoned him,"

"Who?"

"The Devil,"

I have to hand it to him, despite the fact that I scoffed and shouted and berated him, he held his composure. Or, at least, what was left of it. He didn't flinch, he didn't argue, he just sat slumped, staring at the hospital tiles whilst fiddling with a loose thread on the chair.

It's all true, the Devil, he's real.

A shadow settled over me, a dark, stifling, irremovable shadow that comes from the knowledge that something malicious and cruel and purely evil exists. That there was nothing I could do about it, like knowing how insignificant you are in the cosmic wilderness that is the universe, or that humanity is slowly destroying itself through war and ignorance. It was something that I could never escape from. A story, a belief coming true. There was no going back.

When I finally fell into silence, my face hot and flushed from my outburst of denials, Dad continued.

"We made a deal. I asked to see my wife again and Huang asked for money and power. In return, we had to kill any communicators, any of those who could communicate with the dead. I thought, how often do they come along? I've never met a single one. So I made the deal at the forfeit of my own soul. Naturally." he said it so lightly, so casually, as if he was forfeiting his pudding for the evening rather than the rest of his existence, "I had my family again, sitting around the breakfast table," he laughed hollowly, "Then who should walk through the door but my daughter's new best friend Cassandra. It wasn't just 'nice to meet you Mr Parker' but 'nice to meet you Mr and Mrs Parker," he practically spat the last word out, bitterness heavy in his voice.

"And I refused to kill her. I didn't tell Huang about her or any of the others when Huang began recruiting. I kept quiet, desperate that no one would notice. But of course he did. I don't know why I thought I could get away with it. It was the last time I saw her, him taking her away again was a warning I think.

"I've tried so hard to keep Cass safe, to stop them finding out about what she could do. But..."

"But that wasn't Cass's style was it?" I finished softly. Cowan gave an appreciative chuckle.

"No, no it wasn't," Dad gave a half-hearted smile but it quickly fell off his face, "And now you can do it. There's no getting out of this,"

I tried to put everything into order in my mind, seeing my mental jigsaw become almost complete. The only bits missing were what we did next. My dream suddenly emerged from the depths of my memory where I had shoved it so I wouldn't have to think about it. It erupted in my mind's eye in a kaleidoscope of depressing blues, greys, shadows and ghosts. The three teenagers.

"Have you actually ever killed anyone?"

Silence.

Then-

"I didn't stop it,"

"How many?"

"Three,"

I couldn't look at him. Those poor kids. They were like me, like Cowan, like Cass. The kids that didn't quite fit in with what was expected of them from the school heiarchy, who weren't like everyone else. Oh, so what if they could talk to the dead? So what if they weren't like you? That didn't mean they deserved to die.

"How...?" I stumbled over my words, each one fighting to get out. A mixture of swearing, insults, anger, demands, tears, disbelief, horror. But amongst all that noise and passion and emotion, there wasn't a single "I forgive you," He had started all of this, this madness. He had killed, or at least allowed it to happen. He was the reason that the people I loved were dead.

Then suddenly Cowan was beside me and it devastated me that the sheet didn't crease in the slightest beneath his weight. They were both beginning to fade I noticed, one moment they appeared solid, real, very much alive, the next I could make out the chair through Mum, the bedsheets through Cowan's legs.

Dad got up and left, unable to take the pressing silence of the room, muttering to himself, his eyes filling with tears again.

Coward.

Mum and Cowan faded until I couldn't see them anymore, until I couldn't even sense their presence.

I was left alone.

Chapter 17

It was a week later before I finally surfaced into some sort of reality again. They let me out of hospital the following Tuesday, having kept me in for an extra two days just to "double-check" that I was better since my medication didn't seem to be having an effect. That was because my medication had mysteriously found its way into the toilet at the end of the corridor. It was a dangerous game to play I knew, I was seriously ill, but I mistrusted Huang so much that I was willing to take that risk.

I went to school for one day, thinking that it would take my mind of things, but I spent most of my time staring out of the window, dodging Courtney and Blake and trying not to sob whenever I saw Cowan's empty seat. After ignoring the third summons to O'Donnell's office and finding him prowling the corridors for me at lunch, I gave up and went home.

I mooched around for the rest of the week, rarely leaving my room. At night, I hid in my bed, listening to music to block out any of the noises and chanting that crept between the cracks of my window. I think Dad slept outside my room each night, but I couldn't be sure.

Today was Thursday 30th. It was already getting dark, and I had barely moved from staring at the ceiling. Dad had tried speaking to me, encouraging me to get up, do something productive, or at least take a shower.

I turned my back on him, my silence being, I thought, an obvious answer. Instead he said, "Halloween tomorrow," as he left the room, "You excited?"

That was a mildly inappropriate thing to say after what I had just gone through, wasn't it?

That had been three hours ago and I had heard him settle in front of the TV again, most likely gorging on poptarts. Since then, I hadn't moved, sinking further into my mattress and my own self-pity.

That was until two minutes ago. Since Cowan and Mum had vanished, I hadn't seen her, hadn't heard a single word from her. I hadn't heard from any of them. They had all vanished and for the first time in ten years, I was living like everyone else. I had no communications with them, my mind was my own, the dead were dead and there was nothing I could do about it.

God did I hate it.

I had sunk into a deep dark hole of depression, everything was monochromatic and blurred and dull. I thought the only way out was to join them, then at least I wouldn't have to live in fear, constantly avoiding my headmaster, my doctor, my Dad. Every heavy thought that was dragging me down, that was drowning me, would be gone. I would be lighter, free. I wouldn't be alone.

It was as I had that precise thought that it happened. I had been lying in bed, happily stuck in the body-shaped hole of my mattress when the same crack in the corner of the ceiling that had been a blurred line for the past three days suddenly snapped into focus. I glanced around my room nervously, the dim light of the streetlight outside suddenly too bright. It was no longer orange, but bright white. My room was a myriad of colours and lights. At first I thought I was dying, that my concussion had finally caught up on me.

But no-

This couldn't be it, it couldn't be death. This was too beautiful. My whole room was alive.

And I realised that maybe, when it really came down to it, I wasn't ready to give up quite yet.

"You came back," Cass was standing in the centre of what seemed like a hurricane of clarity. It was indescribable how she pulled everything into focus, highlighted the things of beauty and ignored the things that weren't.

Classic Cass. Acting as if the obstacles weren't even there.

"After everything I said to you, after everything I did. That night, you came back when I realised about Cowan..."

'Yes. I'm sorry. I'm sorry I lied, I'm sorry that I couldn't do anything to help you then.'

Her mouth didn't move. Her ghost just stood there, calm and collected as the world whirled into focus around her. Small details became blindingly obvious, like the singular threads in my pyjamas that had been pulled apart by the thorns and branches of the forest, or the small particles of dirt trapped between them, the faint bruising that still stretched across my knuckles and each individual freckle on Cass's face. She was back in my mind, and my brain fizzled with electricity.

It was such a relief.

'You have to help us.'

"I... I tried," I paused, thinking of what I had promised Cowan. I promised that he would get into uni and that he would buy a house and my chest constricted. I'd already broken the first two within a matter of hours, so I turned to the third. 'We're gonna get Cass and those kids some sort of peace.' Had I tried? Had I really, or had I just sulked and argued and only tried to save myself?

"Okay, I didn't try," I amended, "Not properly anyway. But what do I need to do?"

'Stop them.'

"That really helps me Cass,"

'Tomorrow night is their final night. They have my blood, they have Cowan's. They need one more child's and then it will all go down.'

A final showdown. Of course, what else? Tomorrow was Halloween, or more precisely, All Hallow's Eve, wasn't it? There would be hundreds of kids on the streets ripe for the picking. If we didn't stop them tomorrow, what were they going to do next year, or the year after that? They were more powerful now than they had ever been before, I couldn't begin to fathom what they might be capable of getting away with.

'You need your Dad's help-'

"What? I can never look at my father again, nevermind talk to him!"

What Cass said next was the longest thing I ever heard or will ever hear her say. It all came out in a tumble of words, that swept through my mind in a wave.

'You don't understand. When he saved you, when he picked you up when you were bleeding and… and dying he was wild. He went absolutely mental, yelling and bellowing and telling all these murderers how wrong they were and how stupid they had been for believing that they would receive anything for murdering teenagers. He tried to save Cowan, Mel, he tried so bloody hard. You got away from that clearing, you and Cowan were so close to getting away completely. You were at the car but, your Dad, he's only one man. Cowan, the complete and utter twit, went back because if he hadn't, they would have got your Dad, and they would have got you.'

She had faded quite a bit by then, my room had dimmed and the dull glimmer of the orange streetlight overtook my room in a gloomy glow, no longer the vibrant sunset it was seconds ago. I realised we had been talking for far too long, night had fallen completely. We were running out of time.

'Open yourself up, let us back in.'

"Wait, what do you mean? Cass? Cass!" but she had faded to nothing but a transparent shadow.

I was lucky to break through, her words were a whisper now, so close to the edge of my hearing. I started to panic, my heart pounding an erratic rhythm at the thought of losing her again. My memories of the past two weeks came flooding in, wiping out every other clear thought. I couldn't do this alone, I needed Cass, I needed Cowan, I needed my Mum. Each face loomed into my vision, only to be replaced by the blurred images of O'Donnell and Huang, Berkeley and his traitorous children.

"Cass!"

'Focus.'

That was the last word she left me with. It took me a few minutes to calm down and steady my breathing and actually think about what Cass had told me. The story of Cowan and Dad was too painful to comprehend yet, so I filed it away for later. I had to think about what to do next, to form a plan that would stop them. But my mind was blank, I really needed help. As much as I was grateful for Cass's visit, she hadn't told me very much in the way of stopping them.

Open yourself up: sounds dangerous.

Let us back in: as if I was actively trying to block them out!

And focus: I was focused, I was focusing right now… I squeezed my eyes shut but Berkeley's leering face ballooned in front of my eyes and I saw Cowan, broken and bleeding…

Cass was right, I was too easily distracted, to easily pulled away from the important things that I should be doing. Like stopping these people. I pulled a sweater over my head and glanced at the clock: 6:01. We used to love Halloween, the three of us, and we would always dress up as the same things every year because we couldn't think of anything better. Cass would be a witch, naturally, and Cowan would be a pirate who had to draw on the beard with Cass's eyeliner since he could never grow one. I would always dress as a ninja and would wrap a pair of tights around my head. Even when we got too old for trick or treating, we would still dress up.

It was tradition.

I felt a familiar ache in my chest but I was beginning to get used to it. This was a pain that was never going to go away.

I pushed my door open a tiny bit, tentatively peering out into the dark landing, half-expecting to see a cloaked figure. That would make things a lot easier if they came to me, but no, it was just the shadow of the tree outside. I pushed my door open further with more force and it smacked against something solid and unyielding. I flinched, jumping back into my room before peering out cautiously again when nothing else happened. My door had bumped into Dad's favourite armchair which he had somehow lugged up the stairs and placed just outside my room. It had a pillow and blanket strewn across it so I guessed he had been sleeping there. I couldn't believe I hadn't noticed it before, how long had it been there?

I darted across the landing and down the stairs, feeling uncomfortable in the darkness despite it being punctuated by the odd orange rectangle from the streetlamp outside. The TV was blaring and I could hear the tinny laughter. Peeking in I saw Dad lounging on the sofa, the TV causing his face to flash white and black, pink and blue creating deep crevices in his face. He was tapping quick and rhythmically on the sofa's arm. He seemed terrifying, but then I noticed the two empty poptart boxes on the floor at his feet and a third half empty one at his side, the half-drunk beer bottle and the crumbs all the way down his front.

I blurted out, "You mess," before I could stop myself.

Dad practically jumped out of his skin, crumbs flying and beer spilling everywhere. He swore loudly, "You made me jump," he accused, "Do you have to sneak up on me like that, as if I'm not on edge enough already,"

"Wait, you're on edge?" I retorted indignantly, "How do you think I-" I stopped, the pointless argument I'd had with Cowan leaping to the forefront of my mind. What if this was the last time I saw Dad? He is a terrible person yes, but he also raised me, basically, single-handedly. He was the only person I had left. I had to be careful that I didn't lose him too.

"What, what about you Mel?" he argued, scowling without taking his eyes off the screen, still tapping but more erratically now, "It's always about you Mel isn't it?"

I buried my hands in my sweater's pocket to hide the fact that my hands were clenched and shaking with anger. But I couldn't deny it, I had always been selfish. But not this time.

"Have you been sleeping outside my room?" I asked instead.

"Yes," he admitted grudgingly, "I don't trust them, I'm worried they'll break in,"

"Ah,"

"I've also been looking at new homes," he said quickly, getting the words in a hurry out before I could argue, "In far, remote places because we aren't safe here and I need to think about how to get out of it utterly and completely,"

I didn't say anything. Part of me agreed wholeheartedly with him, I couldn't go on avoiding all the influential people here and it would be safer. Why would they bother to come after us? But the small, stubborn part of me argued that this was where I grew up, this was where my friends were. I needed to help them. I wasn't ready to leave them just yet.

"I need to keep you safe kiddo,"

"I suppose going out to take them down tonight isn't a good way to keep me safe?" I suggested nervously. He stared at me and finally stopped tapping. His eyes were bloodshot and I didn't think that the beer he had spilled on the carpet was his first.

"What the hell are you talking about?"

"I- I promised Cowan," I stuttered, fumbling with my words, staring at my barefeet, "Promised that I would find those kids some peace and I think the only way to do that is to stop them. What better night to do than tonight, right?"

"No," straight, flat, absolutely not.

"But-"

"No, go back to your room Mel," he turned back to the television, his eyes dead, twitching and tapping, "And start thinking about packing,"

I opened my mouth to argue but I hesitated, watching him as he started muttering to himself, running a hand through his hair and then roughly pulling it away when it got stuck in his curls. His knee was bouncing up and down and his fingers simply wouldn't stop moving.

"Dad, are you okay?"

He waved me away, his hand jerking back and forth, "Fine, fine,"

"Alright Dad," I sighed, backing away slowly, furious with him and disappointed and pitying. He wasn't going to be of any help so I turned around and headed for the stairs. But instead of trudging up them, I paused staring up into the darkness.

I had never seen him like that. Not ever. His unusual behaviour unnerved me, he didn't really drink all that much because when he did he would get drunk too quick and then wake up with hangovers that would floor him. And the fact that he couldn't stop moving. There was something terribly wrong and I knew there was nothing I could do about it.

Knowing there was nothing I could do, I turned to the immediate problem at hand. I need to figure out a way to stop them. I needed a plan, one that I could do alone and that could be completed within twenty four hours.

Easy.

I thought about what Cass said to me, about them having everyone's blood and preparing for one final showdown. If I wanted to make any impact at all, I needed to be there, right where the action was happening.

I began to climb the stairs slowly, an idea forming in my mind. If Dad could make a deal, anyone could right? Was there a way to make a deal with the Devil so that Dad could get his soul back, so that he could be forgiven, so that everyone could be at peace? What could the price for that possibly be? I reached the top of the landing, and for the first time, I realised I didn't care. I was willing to do anything to save everyone. Especially Cass and Cowan. Maybe Dad if I had the time.

I couldn't possibly ask Dad about contacting the Devil, but there were a few other people I could try. I hurried into my room, flipping open my laptop and rapidly opening facebook. The computer screen lit up my room in an eerie blue glow, but its brightness didn't bother me in the slightest. I clicked on Blake's face. He was the last person I wanted to talk to, but he was perhaps the best person to convince into letting me join. It was stupid and short-sighted, and I hadn't really thought it through. How on earth could I trust him after how he had lied to me?

I hesitated for a moment before typing: 'I want to join. I've got nothing left to lose and I'm only looking out for myself now. This seems to be the option that will most benefit me.'

He must have been sitting next to his phone or something because his reply was instantaneous, and his words made my stomach twist in anger: 'You haven't got the guts.'

I tapped the table top, wondering what I would have to say to convince him. I ran through a few excuses, none of them seeming particularly plausible. In the end, I settled on the truth, or at least something close to it. 'I'll be honest, I want to make my own deal.'

Again, his reply was instant and I wondered if it was just him on the other end. 'Why are you telling me?'

I sighed frustratedly, annoyed that I had to admit that I didn't know how. 'Because I need your help in summoning him and things.'

'Why would I help you? So that you can betray me when you make the deal?'

I stared at the screen for a while, seeing each individual pixel of the screen blur into one another. I had nothing to offer him, nothing substantial enough to convince him. I reread the message several times, the second question nagging at me. I began to type back an answer slowly but picked up the pace as everything fell into place. 'I'll include you in the deal so that you don't lose anything, so that you can only benefit.'

All that he replied with was: 'meet me at my garage tomorrow at nine sharp.' I didn't know if he believed me or not.

Chapter 18

I glared at my phone, irritated that it already read 9:22. Admittedly I had been five minutes late because I had to avoid a hungover father who was struggling to make himself a cup of coffee in the kitchen, but this was getting ridiculous. I had messaged him three times as well and he still chose to ignore me and I was ready to turn back home, my plan falling to pieces before me already when he finally appeared.

The sight of him caused my breath to catch and I had to stop of myself from screaming obscene insults at him. He seemed so laid-back and unimpressed, as if everything that had happened meant nothing to him. He was nothing like he had been last week. That passionate and enraged boy who was willing to do anything to help Cass was gone, only an emotionless asshole remained.

"You sure you want to do this?" he asked sceptically, and I was surprised he was willing to go through this with me of all people.

"Yes," I responded stonily, determined to be just as emotionless and uncaring as he was.

"You better come in then," he said turning round and heading back through the garage. I hesitated, knowing that I couldn't trust him, that this was probably one of the most stupidest things that I'd ever done, possibly on the same level as charging into a group of devil worshippers mid-ritual.

"No one else is in, if that's what you're worried about," he called over his shoulder.

"Nah, I'm just worried about you," I muttered, but I followed him anyway. He took me through the garage then kitchen, past the dining room where the disastrous meal had taken place and into a study across the hall on the ground floor. I could just make out a small, red shadow still on the marble floor of the hall.

Inside the study it was small and cramped. A great mahogany desk took up the space beneath the window with a plush armchair placed behind it. Whoever sat there, as a result, was cast into shadow because you were blinded by the sun streaming through the south-facing window behind it. The other two walls were lined with shelves, filled with aging leather-bound books and random knick knacks such as candles and photo frames and figurines that were all lined with a thin film of dust. Berkeley had also seen fit to squeeze in a giant, sepia-toned antique globe that took up most of the space left in the room. To make things worse, piles of paperwork were balanced precariously everywhere in such a way that the slightest breeze would topple them and send the room into chaos. As if the room wasn't in chaos already.

I tried to ignore the heavy green and brown colour scheme of the room and focused on Blake as he pulled a particularly large and battered leather bound book from a top shelf.

"This," he puffed, "is basically all you need to know about everything. It includes every ritual, including the one you need," He dropped it unceremoniously onto the desk with a thump and the papers wobbled worryingly.

"Thanks," was all I could say.

He flicked through until he was near the end of the book. I came and leaned over his shoulder, slightly awed by the yellowed pages and the knowledge they contained, despite the fact that it was knowledge about worshipping the Devil. I peered closer at the writing, wondering if it was because the pages were so withered with age that I couldn't understand the inked writing.

But no. It was in Latin.

"What the hell, I can't read that!" I complained.

"For translation services, you have to make the deal with me," How about no. He whipped out a crumpled piece of paper from his back pocket and handed it to me and I realised how little this meant to him.

"You go an E in GCSE French but you can read Latin?" I asked sceptically.

"Greek actually," he said, shrugging and his lack of attention was starting to get on my nerves. I sat in the great armchair and scanned through what was written on the paper:

By signing this contract, I, Melanie Parker, agree to the terms laid out. In my contract with Father of Lies/King of Babylon/Lucifer I promise to use the phrase 'Raven Wood Worshippers' for all participants of the group and to exclude Blake Howard Berkeley in said group. Any benefits I may receive, he will also receive in equivalence. Dishonouring this agreement results in the forfeit of my own soul.

"Raven Wood Worshippers?" I asked as he placed an ink pot and feather next to me, "Seriously?" I raised an eyebrow.

"This," he said, indicating the feather and ink, "is tradition and the Raven Wood Worshippers is the group that your Dad and Huang created together and that my father now leads," he said it with some pompous and superiority, and I couldn't help but think about what Dad had become. He had created a powerful group of people, led them for ten years, and now he was succumbing to alcohol and his own depression and was being scorned by a pothead. I suppose he deserved it but it still made my blood boil to hear his drawl.

"By signing this and not including me in them," he continued, "You can cut the entire group out and I am still protected,"

"How did you know that's what I wanted to do?" I asked suspiciously.

"You're pathetically easy to read, like Cass," he laughed, trailing a finger across a shelf and leaving a trail of dust motes dancing in the air, "I'll sign after you so I know you haven't changed anything,"

I stared at the paper before me, my brain in overdrive, desperately trying to figure out what I could possibly do that would include Blake. I couldn't leave him out, I couldn't let him get away with it. After what he said to me when he was about to kill me, after what he done to Cass, he was the one I wanted revenge on the most.

I was about to sign hopelessly, furious with myself for being so stupid, when he said something that changed everything, "Put a few pieces of paper under it. That ink always goes through and I don't wanna get yelled at for ruining the table, y'know?"

I nodded, taking a few blank pieces of paper and placing them neatly beneath the original contract. An idea formed in my head and my hands were already shaking with the thought of it. Blake had been so lazy that he had written the contract on cheap printer paper that was super thin. So thin that the ink was guaranteed to go through.

I glanced up, Blake was entranced by what appeared to be a rat's skull that for some reason beyond my comprehension Berkeley had thought appropriate to have mounted. I quickly scrawled on the paper beneath his contract, ignoring the sickening jolt I felt when the ink came out red:

By signing this contract I, Blake Howard Berkeley, agree to any contract that this contract is attached to, regardless of any previous contracts signed.

I carefully lined the papers up again and signed my name in neat letters: Melanie Anne Parker.

"Okay, all done," I went to move out of the seat, but Blake simply leaned over me and I had to sit there, trapped in his musk of sweat and cigerette smoke. I nervously watched as he rechecked his deal, begging to whatever God there was that he wouldn't notice the red shadow letters beneath his.

His hesitation was beginning to stretch and my leg started to bounce nervously, "You remember how to spell you name right?" I mocked, "Because I don't think I could take being next to your armpit for much longer,"

The jibe struck a chord with his pride rather than his suspicion and he angrily scratched his name into the paper. The letters lay bright and wet on the paper and I had to turn away before I heaved up the little breakfast I had managed to eat.

"What do I do then?"

Blake stretched, dropping the feather next to the pot and spraying a spatter of... whatever it was across the desk top. He stood opposite me and leaned over the book, "Do you want to take notes?"

"Uh," I was dumbfounded for a second, hardly believing that this was actually happening, that he was willing to give me all the information, "Yeah. You got a normal pen?"

He snorted and threw a ballpoint at me. I folded up the top two pages and tucked them into my own hoodie pocket but Blake didn't seem to care that I had his contract. It didn't matter to him anymore. I was delighted to see that 'Blake Howard Berkeley' was faintly visible on the page that was third from the top. I told him I was ready and Blake began to read.

Chapter 19

Hours later I was standing in the doorway leading to the living room again. I was watching Dad, sitting on the sofa, staring mindlessly at the TV again with abandoned poptart boxes and beer bottles. Some were old ones from last night, others new and freshly pulled apart. I had been staring at him for a while, too scared to say anything. His eyes were glassy and he was completely still. The only problem was that the television was paused.

I had the notes from Blake this morning clutched in my hands because a thought had occurred to me. I couldn't understand a single work in that book he had read from, what with it being completely written in Greek. How was I to know that what he had told me was true? That he hadn't changed some vital word or phrase during the ritual that would get me killed? I had resolved to ask Dad but I had been standing here for fifteen minutes, far too terrified to even broach the subject with him.

Eventually it started to get dark and I knew I would have to go meet Blake at the church, which would take a while because I needed to walk. Once again, I knew I was making a massively irresponsible decision but apparently that place had the best so-called 'connection' and the others weren't getting there until late into the night apparently.

I didn't believe Blake in the slightest. The instructions were arduous and ridiculous. I just needed to make sure that what I was doing was right. And I suppose I owed it to Dad to let him know where I was in case I never came home.

I could hear children's shouts of laughter outside and the rattling of candy inside plastic pumpkins. Halloween was beginning. But none of them stopped to call at our house, most likely because it was drenched in darkness at the moment and it looked like no one was home. I felt strange without my childish costume, it was my first year without it.

I drew myself up to my full height, a pretty measly height but my full height all the same, took a deep breath and said loudly and authoritatively, "Dad, I need to speak to you,"

"Huh?" he emerged from whatever stupor he had sunk into, looking vaguely around in bewilderment as he tried to figure out where he was.

"I need you to check something for me, but you can't get mad okay?"

"Uh,"

"Promise?"

"Mnh,"

This wasn't particularly reassuring. I took a step into the living room and it stank of BO and beer, so much so that I held my hoodie sleeve over my nose, "Jesus Dad, what have you been doing?"

His head lolled back as he stared at me through glazed eyes and he spoke thickly, as if his tongue was too heavy for his mouth, "Drinking,"

"Well, maybe you shouldn't drink anymore," I moved further into the lounge, looking around at the ravages of beer bottles and crumbs and ripped pieces of cardboard as a result of Dad's recent descent into despair. I couldn't see any more full beer bottles however, he must have managed to finish them all off.

He didn't reply, just rubbed his arm across his eyes and sighed. I forged on, part of me hoping that this detached state of his would mean he wouldn't really realise what I was about to do, "Can you check this over for me, make sure it's all correct?" I held the crumpled piece of paper in front of his face and he stared at it for a few seconds, squinting in the semi-darkness.

"What is this?" he said, suddenly worryingly sober. He snatched it out of my hands and threw it on the fire. Luckily, it wasn't lit and it just rested lightly on top of the coals. I picked it back up and kept it out of his reach.

"You know what it is," I responded quietly, staring at my feet.

"What- why-" he could barely get his words out and I wasn't sure if it was because he was slurring due to the alcohol or because he was really angry, "How could you be this stupid?" He got to his feet, or at least stumbled to them precariously, "Give it here,"

I stared up at him, my father, who I had always assumed to be that tall, intimidating, influential man that everyone admired but who was actually lonely, pathetic and terrified. "No," I said simply.

"You have no idea what you're getting into," he growled, making another snatch but his movements were slow and blundering, inhibited by the alcohol that must have entirely replaced his bloodstream by now. I easily side stepped, backing away to the hall.

"I do," I argued, but even to me my voice sounded whiny. He was right, I didn't know what I was getting myself into, I couldn't begin to comprehend it. The only thing I was certain of was that I had to do this, and of course, there was that small, minuscule loophole...

"I'm going to do it anyway," I continued, "You're not going to stop me. The least you could do is make sure it's right so it doesn't all go to hell before I even start!"

"It's all going to hell anyway!" he yelled.

"Oh so it's hell either way? Then where's the difference?" I retorted. We both stood there in the semi-darkness, bathed in the luminescent glow of the television. He was breathing heavily, struggling to control his anger, struggling to control anything. He slumped back down on the sofa, head in his hands. It occurred to me that what I had said was selfish, that I hadn't thought for a moment about how he might feel about the prospect of losing me. Then again, I doubt he thought about the families who had lost their children too because of him.

After a minute or so of waiting in a terribly awkward silence, I figured he wasn't going to help. It was as I was turning away that he flicked the lamp whilst simultaneously flicking off the television, a move I didn't think he was capable of. I blinked a few times against the shining, yellow light.

"Give it here, let me see," he said, defeated.

"You're not going to rip it up, are you?"

"Only if you go make me a coffee,"

After a few seconds hesitation, I handed over the few pages and went into the kitchen to make coffee. It only took a few minutes and I bought him a glass of water through too in the hope that it might sober him up slightly. When I finally returned with his black coffee and water, he was leaning over the table, a red pen in his hand correcting the pages. He was tutting like a school teacher who was particularly disappointed in a student, one that he had had high hopes for but who had ended up winging the test because they were lazy.

"I'm assuming this was translated from Grimoire Apollyon right?"

I started at him blankly, "Possibly,"

"Big leather book, written in Greek," he described vaguely.

"Sounds about right,"

"Yeah well, whoever you got to translate it needs to work on their Ancient Greek," he sighed, scratching out another word in red pen and writing the correct one above it.

I couldn't hold back the smug little smile, "How come?"

"Well, first it's 'διάβολος' which is pronounced diábolos not Diabolos," he began.

"What's the difference?" I interrupted.

"Well, one is loosely translates as 'Devil' or 'Satan' in Ancient Greek the other is the little circus hourglass yo yo thing that's not on strings,"

My blank look didn't falter.

Dad continued, falling into University Tutor mode, "Secondly, you only need the once circle on the floor so all these pentagrams are kind of irrelevant. It's showboating and time-consuming. The only other thing you need is the sigil which is one of the few things they've managed to get right. And candles, you don't need this many candles, jesus!" he exclaimed, "Where in hell's name are you going to get six hundred and sixty six candles from?"

I shrugged, my heart thumping at the thought that these instructions were so riddled with mistakes. Had Blake done it on purpose? All the mistakes were expensive and meant I would probably run out of time to complete it. I hoped that Blake was just dumber than he thought, but the thought of screwing this ritual up still made me feel sick.

"I mean, the bonfire is usually enough, it releases the same amount of energy, if not more so," Dad's eyes were bright, and it worried me that he was beginning to enjoy this, "You're performing it where they do, aren't you?"

I nodded reluctantly, "Apparently they're not showing until midnight,"

"Is that from the same source who translated this?"

"Yes,"

He handed the pages back and downed the glass of water and then the coffee before saying, "I'm going to be there for you, one because I don't trust this guy and two because I've screwed things up with you enough times," he held a hand up as I began to argue, "No, I haven't looked after you properly what with being wrapped up in myself and…. other things. I won't make it obvious, but I will be there. And anyway," he added, "I've got my own things to sort out once and for all,"

Chapter 20

Twenty minutes later I sat, swinging my legs, in exactly the same spot I had sat with Cowan at Cass's funeral. I sensed that I was close to the end of this, that things had finally come full circle. I was chipping paint of the sign with my heels again, watching it drift to the floor like dust mites in my torchlight.

Dad had dropped me off and quickly driven away, muttering to himself about forgiveness and how driving under the influence was just one more sin to add to the list. I had a backpack filled with lighters and newspaper to help me start the fire as well as a squirty bottle of incense that we had improvised. Dad had also given me pepper spray in case things got a little hairy.

It was as I had been waiting for ten minutes, Blake late as usual, that it occurred to me that to do this I didn't actually need Blake. It was something that I was capable of doing alone. Blake couldn't sabotage the ritual in any way if he wasn't there and at least if I was moving towards the circle of graves, I wasn't a sitting duck. I could have had a flashing arrow with sparkling lights above my head and been less of a target.

I jumped from the wall and started to run, my backpack bumping against the small of my back and my torch dancing over gravestones. I saw my mother's grave flash by and briefly wondered where they were going to bury Cowan or whether he was going to be cremated. With a flash of horror, I realised that I didn't actually know. What kind of person did that make me?

I hurtled into the forest, heading straight for the little path that was hidden on the right. It took me a few minutes to find it and when I did I had to slow to a brisk walk to avoid being torn to shreds. It was dark and misty, like the first night Cowan and I visited here. Fog hung suspended between branches and swirled in on itself as I brushed past. It curled around trunks and settled on me, leaving me damp and shivering. Looking up, I could barely see the sky, barely see the tops of the trees even because the fog was so thick. I squinted, looking ahead, struggling to see anything in the darkness. I was sure there was no fire burning which was good for me, it meant that no one was there yet.

I staggered and tumbled forwards, repeatedly losing my balance on the loose dirt and tree roots. If Cowan had been here, he would have been helping me up despite the laughing and regardless how many times I fell down. Cass simply would have been bent over with laughter, completely useless. It made me smile to think about them, to think that whatever danger I was heading into they wouldn't have hesitated to have come with me.

I slipped again and a small scream escaped as I fell back and blindly groped for a branch. I managed to grasp one, frozen mid fall, my mind filled with images of the first time I fell here and cracked my head against a rock. And the second time I came here and my head was smashed open again. I resolved that this time was the third time lucky and I wouldn't hit my head. I stood, tentatively touching the gammy spot that was only just beginning to scab over at the base of my skull. It had healed a bit, but the scar would be there forever.

I forged on, ignoring the intermittent spasms of pain from the base of my skull. I shouldn't have touched it, I'd made it worse. It was as I was worrying over my scab that I heard it. A twig snap a few metres to my right.

I froze, shining my torch into the darkness, straining my eyes for the outline of a hooded and cloaked figure. But I couldn't see anything but the mist, reflecting my torchlight back, practically blinding me. I began to move cautiously forward, not taking my eyes off the mist beside me. This caused me to trip several times more than usual, so I settled on regularly glancing to my right.

Then, as my heartbeat finally settled to a rhythm that somewhat resembled calm, it happened again. Three sharp snaps! in quick succession, coming closer. I swore under my breath, trying to breathe, when they began to snap faster and faster, closer and closer. Mercifully, I unfroze and my instincts kicked in, my body naturally choosing flight over fight. I hurtled through the trees, gasping as they slapped against me. I wasn't about to be caught and strangled again. I didn't have Cowan here to save me this time.

I was running, so fast and panicked that my knees almost buckled beneath me on every step. I couldn't see where I was going because of the mist and because it had plastered my hair against my forehead and so trees continually slapped me in the face. And I could hear them behind me, there were dozens of them, all running after me and my head was pounding and I couldn't see and I was losing my footing and suddenly I was tumbling, falling through the air-

And I landed, rolling into the middle of the clearing, gasping for breath and staring up at the first bit of clear sky I had seen all night. My breath formed crystallised clouds just above me and I thought of the time that Cass and I used to play dragons and pretend it was smoke coming out of our noses.

The noises following me had stopped.

I sat up, searching the forest for signs of them, for anyone at all but the surrounding trees were deserted. The mist hung at the edges of the clearing, as if there was an invisible threshold it couldn't cross. A pile of ash showed where the fire was usually lit so I quickly pulled everything out my backpack, shivering with the cold and desperate to get the fire lit. The fire would illuminate the entire area. It would be better than my torch, which could only spotlight and which plunged everything else around into further darkness.

There was a convenient pile of logs I found, behind one of the tombs. There were suspicious marks splattered all over it and I couldn't bear to look at it. All I could think about was Cowan and Cass and how awful and how lonely-

Snap!

"For God's sake, who's there?" I demanded, dropping all the logs in fright. I stared defiantly into the darkness, trying to hide my uncertainty over who could be out there. I quickly gathered the scattered logs and piled them beside the ashes, building a small pile of newspapers and then fumbling with the lighter in the darkness.

Snap!

I tried the lighter again and only succeeded in burning my thumb, "Bloody hell,"

Snap!

"Yes yes yes!" Finally, a tiny flame flickered into life and I held it against the rolls of newspapers. They quickly caught, and the fire spread, devouring the paper and leaving only charred remains behind. I gently blew on it and piled small sticks on top before piling on the larger ones. It was as I was leaning over the little fire, speaking to it, encouraging it, that Blake spoke.

"Why didn't you wait?"

I flinched and dropped the lighter into the centre where I heard the plastic crack due to the heat. "Crap," I crawled back and quickly got my feet, grabbing my backpack so that it was out of reach of Blake. The corrected pages were in there, and I wasn't about to let him near them.

"I was only lighting the fire, jeez," I lied as the lighter exploded in the heart of the fire and flames whooshed and reached for the sky. I felt the warmth on my face, even though I was a few metres away.

"I said to wait," he responded, crouching beside the fire and lighting a cigarette.

I sighed, exasperated, "And you're always late," I started to draw a circle in the dirt with the heel of my trainer around the fire and Blake stood and watched me, puffing away, his face bathed in a golden glow that emphasised his acne.

His silence unnerved me, so I awkwardly tried to fill it, "Did you have to be so noisy coming through the woods?" I said as I moved in front of him, deliberately excluding him from my wonky circle.

"Huh?" he asked, surprised.

"Snapping twigs and stuff," I elaborated, completing my circle and pulling the pages and incense from my bag. I also slipped the pepper spray into my pocket along with the secret contract of Blake's.

"I was pretty silent,"

I raised an eyebrow, "Sure you were,"

I double-checked the instructions, despite the fact I had read over them about twenty times in the car on the way here. He also sceptically raised an eyebrow as he took another drag, "You're doing it wrong,"

I began squirting incense above my circle. You were supposed to burn it and swing it in a thurible that had been tainted or something but Dad had leant his to Chief Inspector Stone. How inconvenient.

"Perhaps I'm doing it right and you translated it wrong," I said, squirting him in the face. It made him cough and he scowled as he stumbled back from the pungent smell. His expression confirmed to me that he had done it on purpose. I waved the papers at him, proud of my victory, "I got it corrected, looks like you got a few things wrong,"

Blake dropped his cigarette and crushed it under his boot, "You'll stick to our deal?"

"I can't not, can I?" I placed the pages on the floor and mentally checked off the steps before kicking them out of the circle. It was time to actually begin, and I couldn't help but feel a little ridiculous at the things I was about to say.

With a shaking hand, I drew the Devil's sigil in the air and announced, "I summon thee, the Devil, to this place," There was silence and I blushed, embarrassed.

Blake clapped slowly, "A for effort, very dramatic,"

I flipped him the middle finger and opened my mouth to continue when someone else entered the clearing. Actually, a few people entered and they were the last people I wanted to see.

"Cease this immediately!" Berkeley howled as he flew in, his cloak flapping around his fat thighs and bulging belly. "You must desist with this tainted and unholy ritual!"

Tainted and unholy ritual? Wasn't that the point? I glanced at Blake, "And you call me dramatic," The worshippers circled again and I felt a familiar rush of panic. I could run now, there were still gaps and I could make it out with no harm done. But what would I be going back to? A life on the run where my father could only count down the days until eternal damnation. That didn't sound particularly appealing.

"I request you here sir," I continued, my voice shaking as I ignored Berkeley, "To make a bargain,"

"Stop her Blake!" he roared.

They were moving in and I knew there was no way I was going to be able to finish this before they reached me. There was too much.

Snap!

I stopped. Twigs were still snapping but everyone was already here. I searched the forest edge again as Berkeley picked up my corrected instructions.

"She's changed it, don't you see?" he yelled, "You've failed Blake, she was supposed to complete our ritual so that we could receive her soul and so that we would have power over her father. But you've mucked it up boy, you allowed her to get it corrected!" he seethed, "And by Marcus of all people," he muttered.

I kept my eyes on the trees, straining my ears for another snap of twigs or crackle of leaves, "In return for what I desire, I am prepared to give you what you require," I whispered under my breath, quickly tracing the sigil in the air again and giving another quick spray of incense for good measure.

Blake tilted his head to the side, his hands buried in his pockets. He remained silent beneath his father's onslaught, but he didn't flinch or buckle. He didn't even seem to acknowledge it. The others, however, were at my circles edge and I sprayed them with incense to keep them at bay. It didn't really do anything, but it gave me a chance to squeeze another line in.

"I will support you in your-" Oh god. I faltered, because she was back. She was at the edge of the forest, waving of all things, trying to grab my attention. It was her who had been cracking the twigs, not Blake or the worshippers. I gaped at her, obviously enough that everyone else turned to look too.

"What are you looking at?" Blake asked, half-amused probably at the gormless look on my face.

I turned to gape at him, "You- you-" I felt the same surge of anger that had exploded inside me when he had me pressed against the stone slab all those nights ago.

"You liar," was all I could manage.

"Wha...?" I watched as the realisation dawned on him, "She's here,"

"I thought you, of all people, would know," I growled, trembling with anger, "You never could see her, could you? That was part of all your stupid little lies!"

Berkeley interrupted, "Somebody seize her, stop her from completing the ritual,"

"I will support you in your reign," I said again, trying to get the words out as fast as I could. The tallest of the cloaked figures entered my circle and I felt horribly violated. O'Donnell pulled his hood down and grabbed my wrist, "You should have come to my office when I asked you to,"

I sprayed him with the incense in my other hand, squirting him right in the eyes. He swore loudly as the others surged forwards but were then pushed back again.

"Come on you fools!" Berkeley yelled, waving his hands about as if that would help. O'Donnell flew back and the others were trying, but their seemed to be an invisible barrier between them and me. And invisible barrier that suddenly took the form of Cass, punching and slapping at the worshippers to keep them back.

"Thank you Cass, thank you," Her frizzy red hair was alight in the firelight and she looked so alive, "I've got this, I'm gonna help you,"

I quickly took advantage of her help, "I will honour you in grace,"

Draw another sigil-

Spray some more incense-

Shake the bottle-

Try spraying again-

"I summon you here in fire, storm, or flood,"

A fist came out of nowhere and connected with a resounding crack against my cheekbone. The force of it threw me to the ground and I coughed as blood filled my mouth where I'd bitten my tongue. CI Stone was towering above me and he suited his name, his fist was like a rock. He grabbed me by the collar of my hoodie and hauled me to my feet as I tried to squirt him with incense. Except, I had none left, having used the last of it a few seconds ago.

I shook the bottle and tried again.

A pathetic drizzle escaped the nozzle.

"Shoot,"

Chapter 21

Stone smiled grimly and pulled back his fist to land another blow, when it froze in mid-air. He pushed against the force that was holding him back, but it was too strong. Which was when I saw Cowan with both hands wrapped around Stone's fist, pushing him back. I practically screamed in delight, which startled Stone enough that he dropped me and I got a clear kick at his honoured private parts. All I wanted to do was stop and talk to Cowan, talk to Cass but I knew that to be of any use I would need to finish this. I abandoned the empty squirty bottle and drew the last sigil in the dirt at my feet.

Cowan was now helping Cass and I could see the faint outlines of the others too, those poor teenagers who had suffered the same fate as my best friends.

"And give you my service in return of yours in the form of blood,"

Then-

"Bollocks!"

I had reached the last step and realised I didn't actually have any sharp. There was no way I could seal the ritual with blood. I looked around panicking, annoyed at myself that I could be so stupid and that I wouldn't be able to finish it. Cowan and Cass looked as if they were flicking in and out of existence, solidifying only for long enough to gut punch someone before becoming translucent ghosts again.

Then Dad appeared, hurtling into the clearing and taking out O'Donnell, who was still rubbing his eyes, with a tire iron. Or, at least he did on the third swing. He was still a bit tipsy and struggled to coordinate his improvised weapon from the boot of the car with his eyesight. O'Donnell still crumpled to the floor though, I'll give him that.

They were all working so hard, putting themselves at risk and for what? For me to be a total idiot and forget one of the most important things of the whole flipping ritual.

"Looking for something?" Blake called over the growing pandemonium as worshippers tried to fight off their invisible attackers. He was holding a sharp knife between his fingertips, the blade glinting in the firelight.

Berkeley saw it at the same moment as I did, "Son no! We can solve this! But if you give her the knife, it's all over, there's no telling what she might do!"

Blake tilted his head and I saw that he was nothing like his father. He may share his ambition and ruthlessness, but Blake was cold and calculating, whilst Berkeley was drunk on power, almost as drunk as my father. He had stopped planning ahead, or looking for traitors because he had become so comfortable and secure in his own supremacy.

Berkeley held his hand out in a pacifying motion, "Don't give her the knife Blake,"

Blake paused with the knife and it was only a metre away from me. I could lunge and grab it, finish the ritual before they could do anything about it. In fact, I still had the pepper spray in my pocket, I could easily spray him and anyone else who came near. But Blake's expression stopped me. He was staring at his father with barely disguised disgust.

"Yeah, but the thing is," he said slowly, like he was speaking to an especially stupid child, "if I give to her, I get rid of you,"

I have to admit, Berkeley's reaction was rather amusing. His entire face lost its colour, turning a sickly off-white and his jowls shook. Every crevice and wrinkle and piece of excess fat stood out and his beady, sunken eyes filled with horror at his son's deception.

Then everything moved very quickly. Berkeley threw himself forward at Blake who easily tossed the knife at me. I squealed, attempted to catch the knife but Blake had thrown it too far. It soared past and landed in the dirt on the other side of the circle. Blake swore and Berkeley laughed manically as he switched direction, diving for the knife.

"You've lost! The pair of you!" he screeched as he waved it above his head.

My face was throbbing angrily from where Stone had punched it which gave me an idea. Disregarding all feminine courtesy and dignity, I hacked up a great globule of saliva and spat in Berkeley's direction. The mixture of blood and spit landed perfectly in the circle.

I saw a few worshippers vanish into the woods, self-preservation at the forefront of their minds as they began to register the fact that they were possibly going to lose.

Berkeley lunged forwards, hands out, his face a contorted mask of anger.

I stumbled backwards and away from him, losing my balance-

He grabbed my wrist, twisting-

The pain made my arm spasm-

And I pepper-sprayed him-

And time froze.

I whirled around, gazing in awe at the fact that no one was moving, or more that they were moving extremely slowly. I watched in sickening detail as the pepper spray made contact with Berkeley's eyes and he reacted melodramatically. His face twisted into a grotesque gargoyle, spit flew through the air in an arc over my head, at such a speed that I was able to flick it so that it fragmented into dozens of miniature droplets. It was vile, but fascinating at the same time.

Then somebody coughed to get my attention and I jumped out of my skin. I turned to find a small man in a shabby suit that was slightly too big for him and a briefcase. He looked like a banker down on his luck, his sleeves went past his knuckles and his red tie was loosened like he had been working in a hot office all day. Which, I suppose, he had.

"If you're quite finished, I believe you summoned me," he said briskly, pushing his glasses up his nose. They slipped back down again straight away on sweat, making the movement redundant, "Or at least you summoned the Big Man, but he doesn't appear for little..." he glanced around in distaste at the frozen fight around us, "trivial matters like this,"

"It's very kind of you to appear at all," I responded, my voice strangled. I couldn't believe it had worked; I looked down and saw my blood splattered amongst the dead leaves.

"Yes it was, wasn't it?" he agreed. He opened his briefcase, pulling a few pages that were piled haphazardly and he had to hold his briefcase under his arm as he sorted through them, "Have you a contract prepared?"

"Uh," I mumbled, "Only partially," I pulled out the contract that Blake had unknowingly signed from my hoodie pocket, "This is all I have,"

"Ah," he sighed, irritated, "What do you want then?"

"I, um, I want Cass and Cowan and my mum, those teenagers to be able to rest in peace," I blurted, "And I want to stop the... ah, the... Raven Wood Worshippers from hurting anyone else and-" there was something else, there was something else, "Uh... Dad's soul! I want Dad's soul back. Please," I added.

"Oho, quite the demands," he chuckled, pushing his glasses up his nose again. I stared at him as he scribbled down my demands and began to create my contract. My heart was pounding in my chest as I watched him. His hair was thinning and white and his eyes were an icy grey, like the colour of clouds before a snowstorm. Slate-like, cold, unforgiving.

Finally, after I had nearly bitten my nail off due to nerves, he held out a piece of paper to me:

By signing this contract, Melanie Anne Parker has agreed to the terms regarding Marcus Parker's soul, the peace of Cassandra Hughes, Cowan Micheals, Emma Parker, Leo Browne, Dylan Finn, and Aimee Macready as well as incapacitating the work of the Raven Wood Worshippers excluding those already bound by contracts. Melanie Parker will receive all these things, but in return, the Father of Lies/King of Babylon/Lucifer will receive her soul and the souls of said Raven Wood Worshippers (who have already forfeited their souls in Agreement FFF). She also forfeits her ability to communicate and bear offspring in order to prevent the further continuation of her line of communicators as well as agreeing to eliminate any communicators she may come across. If any of these terms are to be broken, it will result in the prior collection of her soul and the release of the Antichrist, triggering the Apocalypse and dooming the world.

The Antichrist? He watched me as I signed, taking my time. I mean, this, of course, was a monumental decision. Who wouldn't take their time? In actual fact, I was rapidly scribbling adjustments to the page:

...Blake Howard Berkeley has agreed...

...Lucifer will receive Blake's soul....

...he also forfeits his ability...

I subtly attached the piece of paper I had tricked Blake into signing with my favourite stripy paperclip to the contract.

"That's what you get for killing my best friend asshole," I thought, cheerfully handing the contract over. My heart was in my mouth. What would happen if I got caught? What was the punishment for skipping out on your deal? Or putting someone else into one through trickery? The Devil's right hand man smiled knowingly and I think he knew what I'd done. He clicked and the two pieces of paper became one and he handed my favourite paperclip back. It obviously didn't seem to bother him though.

"I like a bit of chaos," he smiled to himself as everyone began to sluggishly move. This was the moment of truth as to whether my plan worked. I could still see Cass and Cowan, but it was still too early to celebrate.

"Oh really?" I respond, conversationally.

He nodded, "Especially when it's chaos for the Big Man,"

I grinned.

We shook hands, coming to a silent agreement between ourselves. His hand, despite being liver-spotted and wrinkled felt as smooth as silk, "It's a good plan. It's nice to see good old fashioned malicious intent isn't dead yet. I'm only going to allow this," he whispered conspiratorially, "this little mix-up in the paperwork because I like you. You have no qualms about sentencing someone to eternal damnation to save your own soul, your selfishness is quite astounding,"

He squeezed my hand so hard that it hurt. I gasped, convinced my bones were going to break when he let go. Hadn't I saved everyone at the same time though? I may have forfeited Blake's soul in order to save my own, but I had also brought Dad's back from the brink of eternal damnation and given peace to the dead. How was I still selfish?

I glared at the man, rubbing the same knuckles I had bruised all that time ago at Cass's funeral when I had clumsily smacked them against a pew. He, in response, simply unfroze time and reality came crashing back with all its noise and its chaos. The brief respite of quiet and calm was swallowed up in a second.

Berkeley was rolling on the floor, clutching his eyes and screaming. I thought it was due to the pepper spray, but then all the worshippers were rolling on the floor and screaming. All the ghosts backed away and stood beside me and for the last time I resumed my space between Cowan and Cass.

We watched the old man take Blake by the arm, holding his bony elbow in a vice-like grip that I knew all too well. I saw his look of confusion, then anger as the old man showed him the contract that he had supposedly signed. He then glared at me, his eyes far more furious and fiery than his father's ever were.

"You broke our deal!" he screamed, spitting and cursing, "You said you would do nothing against me! You liar!"

"I learned from the best!" Technically, I hadn't broken our deal at all. I had promised not to include him under the umbrella of 'Raven Wood Worshippers' which included O'Donnell and Stone and Berkeley who were all currently writhing on the floor and turning to dust. I hadn't included him as part of this group, I had simply made the contract about him.

"I'll kill you!"

"Yeah yeah," I muttered as he was dragged away, still screaming and bucking wildly. The man vanished with a little, insignificant pop! and took Blake with him. The bodies around us disappeared into a final pile of dust so all that was left was me, ghosts, a fire beginning to smoulder and a drunken father stumbling out of the forest, muttering to himself.

There was nothing particularly dramatic about their leaving. It seemed gradual, a slow vanishing of their essence as it moved on. A slight twist and buckle in the wall between worlds that they simply stepped through.

"I'm excited," Cass had grinned wildly, "I mean, except for you guys, this place was a bit crap,"

"I don't want you to go," I'd blurted, "Please,"

"If it's any consolation," Cowan had said, a translucent, glowing lock of hair flopping over his eye, "I don't want to go either,"

"But we don't have a choice," Cass said softly, "This is what you worked for Mel, you can't just throw it away now. It's time to let us go,"

Time to let us go. Could you have thought of anything more clichéd Cass?

Dad had begged for forgiveness, gracefully, I'll give him that. He apologised for his actions, and the actions that had influenced others. He managed to maintain his dignity and pose despite Cass's look of undisguised hatred. Whether he truly redeemed himself I'll never be sure.

Then the door opened. Aimee, Leo and Dylan left first. They seemed to lean forward, taking a single step and-

Gone.

Cass saluted, grinned, said, "I'll see you on the otherside, you better be late,"

Then she took off running, her elbows in her denim jacket pumping like pistons, her slightly chunky thighs racing beneath her skirt, her hair flying and-

Gone.

Cowan was last.

"I love you,"

I didn't dare blink. If I blinked, the tears would escape and I couldn't let that happen.

"I love you too stupid,"

Then, step-

Gone.

Dad, clinging to the tyre iron, "Are they gone?"

I nodded.

"All of them?"

And I realised why he was holding onto that tyre iron so tight. He was clinging on to that one last hope that he would see her again.

And she hadn't even shown.

"I'm sorry Dad," I couldn't tell him but I couldn't lie either. So I stopped, faltering, and he knew.

"I can't blame her," he mumbled, wiping a hand across weeping eyes, "This was never her sort of thing,"

I hiccoughed, a small pathetic acknowledgement of his small pathetic joke.

"Shall we go home?" he murmured.

I nodded.

Chapter 22

We never did see her again. We never saw any of them again. The dead were dead, like they should be. But even Dad noticed that something was lacking, a lustre, an extra dimension to our boringly ordinary lives.

"We have to leave," he said, three days later. We were sitting at the table, two pizzas congealing in front of us, two mugs of coffee growing cold, two souls losing hope.

"Why?"

"Uh, several reasons. Safety, there are still people out there who want us dead or at least eternally damned, I've already booked flights out of the country and I am losing my mind,"

I stared at him, a man who was still hungover three days after his binge. I understood the 'losing my mind' part, I felt like I was trapped in a shell of my former self, like all the little mannerisms and loose thoughts that made me had been flushed out and I was numb. It took and endless amount of energy that I didn't have just to get out of bed.

"What do you mean there are people still out there?" I asked hopelessly. Another major flaw to my flaw-filled plan.

"Not everyone was included. I wasn't, Huang wasn't, there are certain people who weren't officially part of the group, like Courtney for example,"

"Do you remember when you wanted me to be friends with her?"

Dad laughed, "I thought it would keep you safe," he shook his head in disbelief at his own stupidity, "Like, being friends with the daughter of a cultist wouldn't make you a target,"

"And Huang?"

"I lost her in the forest, I don't know why she didn't turn to dust like the others,"

I was too tired to think why.

"We have to leave tomorrow," he said.

"Okay," It was late. I left the table and wandered to my room as Dad returned to his bed for one last night. My bulging rucksack was propped against the wall. By the time he woke up in the morning, I would be long gone. He was right, this house wasn't home anymore. It was full of memories that were faded and colourless and just so empty. There was no one left. Just a murderer and his daughter. A daughter who had already partially followed in his footsteps. If we stayed here, we'd go mad. That was, if we weren't killed first. But I couldn't escape with him. I guess I still hadn't forgiven him.

I pulled on Cowan's coat, the car keys still nestled in the pocket. His funeral had been yesterday, but I hadn't gone. I had missed calls from his parents, practically begging me to come, but I'm ashamed to say I ignored them all. I had said goodbye to him.

I tucked a photo of the three of us into the breast pocket and heaved the rucksack onto my shoulder. I thought about Cowan's stash of alcohol hidden beneath his bed, and how we never got to drink it. The party that never happened. The first kiss I never got. I'd leave now, liberate the Micheals' of Cowan's car for a little while and get as far away as possible. This part of my life, the only part so far, was over. It was time to move on, whether I liked it or not.

Printed in Great Britain
by Amazon